LITTLE LEAGUE®
PERFECT GAME

LITTLE LEAGUE®
PERFECT
GAME

MATT CHRISTOPHER

Little, Brown and Company
New York Boston

Little, Brown and Company

Hachette Book Group
237 Park Avenue, New York, NY 10017
Visit our website at lb-kids.com
mattchristopher.com

Little, Brown and Company is a division of Hachette Book Group, Inc.
The Little, Brown name and logo are trademarks of Hachette Book Group, Inc.

The publisher is not responsible for websites (or their content)
that are not owned by the publisher.

First Edition: March 2014

Matt Christopher® is a registered trademark of Matt Christopher Royalties, Inc.

Little League Baseball, Little League, the medallion and the keystone are registered trademarks and service marks belonging exclusively to Little League Baseball, Incorporated.

© 2014 Little League Baseball, Incorporated. All Rights Reserved.

Text written by Stephanie True Peters

Library of Congress Cataloging-in-Publication Data

Christopher, Matt.
 Perfect game / Matt Christopher. — First edition
  pages cm. — (Little League ; 4)
 Summary: Twelve-year-old cousins—and best friends—Carter and Liam must compete against each other, as players on opposing teams, at this year's Little League World Series.
 ISBN 978-0-316-22045-3 (hardback) — ISBN 978-0-316-24840-2 (ebook)
  [1. Baseball—Fiction.   2. Little League World Series
   (Baseball)—Fiction.   3. Cousins—Fiction.
    4. Friendship—Fiction.]   I. Title.
    PZ7.C458Pe 2014
     [Fic]—dc23
                        2013028252

10 9 8 7 6 5 4 3 2 1

RRD-C

The Little League® Pledge

I trust in God

I love my country

And will respect its laws

I will play fair

And strive to win

But win or lose

I will always do my best

CHAPTER ONE

Liam McGrath, twelve-year-old catcher for the Ravenna All-Stars, had a lot to say to Phillip DiMaggio, the team's top pitcher, but not a lot of time to say it. The first game of the Southern California South Sub-Divisional Tournament was scheduled to begin soon. So he got right to the point.

"True or false: You look at Carter as your rival. So when you found out he and I talk all the time, you didn't like it. That's why you've been giving me the cold shoulder these last few days."

Carter Jones was Liam's cousin. Closer than some brothers, they have shared a love for baseball since the time they could hold bats. Like Phillip, Carter was a talented pitcher. Up until last year, Liam had been his catcher. Then the McGraths moved from Pennsylvania to California. Even though the cousins no longer saw each other regularly, they still talked, texted, and video-chatted all the time.

Phillip crossed his arms over his chest. "True or false," he mimicked. "You guys talked about me."

Liam jabbed the toe of his cleat into the dirt and nodded.

Phillip's piercing black eyes narrowed. "Then the answer to your question is 'true.' I don't like you talking to Carter, and I *really* don't like you talking about me behind my back."

"Yeah, I get that," Liam said. "And I admit some of the stuff I said wasn't very nice. But that was back when I was still bumming out about...this."

He touched his chest with his index finger, then touched his nose and pointed at Phillip.

"There it is again!" Rodney Driscoll, right fielder for Ravenna, said as he trotted over to them, a perplexed look on his chocolate-brown face. Trailing behind him was his brother, Sean, and another boy named Owen Berg.

Liam's lips tightened a bit when he saw Owen. Owen had started out as Phillip's catcher in the postseason. Then an emergency appendectomy sidelined him. Even though he couldn't play, he still wore his cobalt-blue-and-white Ravenna team jersey. Today, he'd be sitting in the dugout with his teammates.

Liam was pretty sure Owen resented him for taking his place at catcher. He didn't really blame him, but he could have done without the cold looks the boy gave him.

Liam turned his attention to Rodney. "There *what* is again?"

"This." Rodney imitated Liam's chest-nose-point gesture. "I've seen both you and Phillip do it. What the heck does it mean?"

"Yeah, I want to know, too," said Sean. Unlike the other boys, Sean wasn't wearing a Ravenna uniform. He hadn't been selected for the All-Star team, nor had he expected to be. He was at every game, though, cheering for the players from the bleachers. "Is that move like a secret signal?"

In a way, Sean was right. The gesture was a signal of sorts, and one only Liam, Phillip, and Carter knew about.

Or so Liam thought until he heard Owen laugh.

"Seriously?" Owen said. "You guys don't know the story behind that? Well, I'll tell it."

Phillip suddenly looked uncomfortable. He cleared his throat. "Yo, IceBerg, I don't think—"

Owen waved him off and addressed the Driscoll

brothers. "So you know Liam's and Phillip's teams played against each other in the U.S. Championship at the Little League Baseball World Series last August. But I bet you didn't know that two nights before that game, Liam played a prank on Phillip."

"You did?" Sean raised an eyebrow at Liam. "What'd you do?"

"I pretended to see a stain on his shirt. When I pointed it out"—Liam tapped Sean's chest to demonstrate—"Phillip looked down and I did this." He flicked Sean's nose with his finger. "Then I pointed at him and said, 'Made you look!' "

Sean laughed. "That's classic!"

"What's classic," Owen cut in impatiently, "is how Phillip got back at him. Bottom of the sixth, Mid-Atlantic is down by one with two outs." He thumped Phillip on the back. "DiMadge here is on the mound for West. Liam comes to the plate. He looks the first pitch into the catcher's glove and fouls the second. The third comes in. He takes a monster cut—and misses completely! He swings so hard that he falls flat on his face!"

Liam flushed to the roots of his brown hair. That strikeout was, hands down, the most humiliating moment of his life.

"Yeah, yeah, we all know about that," Rodney said. "But what does it have to do with that nose gesture?"

"Just this. After Liam strikes out, DiMadge meets him at the plate and does the nose-bop to him. But get this"—Owen started laughing—"instead of saying 'Made you look,' he says, 'Made you whiff!' "

The Driscoll brothers met this statement with dead silence, and for good reason. Liam's nose-bop was a harmless prank. But to mock someone whose strikeout had just ended his team's chances of playing in the title game of the Little League Baseball World Series? Liam could tell that that didn't sit right with Rodney or Sean.

What didn't sit right with Liam was the knowledge that Phillip had told Owen about the incident. He gave the pitcher a hard stare. "Guess I'm not the only one talking behind people's backs." He lifted his chin defiantly, waiting for Phillip to defend himself.

But to his surprise, when Phillip spoke, his voice was full of shame. "Yeah, you're right. And I was wrong, about a lot of stuff." He met Liam's stare. "Taunting you after your strikeout was a lousy thing to do. Bragging about it was even lousier. And intimidating you during the regular season by reminding you of it"—he repeated the nose-bop gesture—"was probably the lousiest of all. I guess what I'm trying to say is, I'm sorry."

Liam was dumbfounded. Dumbfounded, but happy. His embarrassment and resentment evaporated; hope bloomed in their place. Hope that he and Phillip might get back on track as pitcher and catcher. Hope that if they did, Ravenna would win the SoCal South Tournament, and continue on through the Western Regionals, and then to the greatest Little League event of all: the Little League Baseball World Series in Williamsport, Pennsylvania. And he hoped that if they made it that far, they would go all the way to the title game and come back to California as champions.

Feeling as if a tremendous weight had been lifted from his shoulders, he punched Phillip lightly on the arm. "Like you could ever intimidate me."

Phillip's mouth twitched into a half smile. "You saying I didn't?"

"Okay, maybe once or twice," Liam conceded with a laugh. "But that's in the past now, like everything else that's gone down between us. Agreed?"

Phillip's half smile turned into a full-blown grin. "Agreed!"

Rodney stepped between them, wrapped an arm around each boy's neck, and pulled their heads together. "Then what are we waiting for? Let's play ball!"

CHAPTER

Carter Jones opened a drawer in the hotel dresser, took out his T-shirts, and shoved them into his duffel bag. Shorts, swimsuits, and socks followed. He'd just finished packing when someone knocked on his door. He opened it to find his friend and Forest Park teammate Ash LaBrie on the other side.

"Ready to get going?" Ash asked, sticking his foot in the door to hold it ajar.

"Almost. I just need to do one last thing." Carter took out his cell phone and sat down on the hotel bed.

"Who are you calling?"

Carter looked at him. "Who do you think?"

Ash groaned. "Seriously? Why bother? He didn't

want to talk to you. What makes you think he'll talk to you today?"

Carter kept scrolling through his list of contacts. When he reached the one marked LIAM, he hit the call button.

For the last few days, Carter, Ash, and their parents had been staying in a beautiful hotel with an enormous indoor water park. Now they were packing up to head home before going to the Pennsylvania State Little League Tournament. Forest Park was one of eight teams participating.

Carter couldn't wait to get going, although he'd had a great time at the hotel—until the other night, that is. That's when he'd received an e-mail from his cousin Melanie, Liam's sixteen-year-old sister. Attached to the e-mail was a video she had made of clips of Phillip DiMaggio. Melanie was making a documentary of Ravenna's postseason run for a school project, so Carter wasn't surprised she had footage of Phillip. What did surprise him was what the footage revealed.

Ash had spotted it first. "You see that?" he exclaimed while watching the video for the third time. "He's wiping his face on his shoulder."

Carter didn't understand why Ash was so excited until Ash pointed out that Phillip wiped his face before throwing a changeup. Not just now and then, but *every time*. Anyone who knew what to look for would know what pitch Phillip intended to throw.

Ash was convinced that that knowledge could help Forest Park beat Ravenna if the two teams ever met. "Imagine what our batters could do if they knew what pitch was coming!"

Carter's instinct was to tell Liam immediately. But he didn't. For one thing, although it was eight thirty in Pennsylvania, it was only five thirty in the morning California time—too early for Liam to be awake. For another, a very small part of him liked the idea of having an advantage over Phillip.

Carter and Phillip had a long and rocky history that had started two summers before during Little League Baseball Camp. Carter had mistaken Phillip DiMaggio for a descendant of the late, great Yankee Joe DiMaggio. Starstruck, he had asked Phillip to sign his camp jersey. By the time he remembered that Joltin' Joe had no direct descendants, it was too late. Phillip had scrawled *DiMaggio's Number One Fan* on the shoulder in permanent ink. Even worse, he had started calling Carter Number One Fan, much to his friends' amusement— and Carter's embarrassment.

Despite this and the rivalry between their teams at the Little League Baseball World Series the next year, Carter's conscience soon sent the pleasure in having the upper hand over Phillip packing. He called Liam as soon as he could. When he'd tried to explain what he and Ash had discovered, however, Liam cut him off.

Carter had been confused at first. But now he suspected Liam had refused to talk to him because Ash had been in on the conversation.

Liam didn't like Ash. Carter felt bad about that, although he understood the reasons. After Liam moved, Ash had taken over his spot at catcher. Ash had also moved into Liam's former house, played Little League with many of Liam's former teammates, and hung out with Liam's old hometown friends. Add it all up, and Carter guessed he'd feel the same way about Ash if their situations were reversed.

Which, in a way, they were. After all, Liam was now catching for Phillip DiMaggio. Still...

"I don't think it's fair to keep what we know about Phillip from Liam," Carter informed Ash while he waited for Liam to answer.

Ash stepped into the hotel hallway. "And I think you're making a huge mistake." The door closed after him.

A second later, Carter's call was answered, but not by Liam. "The person you are trying to reach is unavailable," a recorded voice informed him.

Carter left a brief three-word message: "Call me, doofus."

CHAPTER
THREE

Liam and Phillip began warming up with some easy throws. Coach Driscoll, Ravenna's manager and Sean and Rodney's father, appeared outside the bull pen a few minutes later.

"I saw you boys talking earlier," he said, taking off his glasses and wiping them on the corner of his jersey. "Everything okay?"

Coach Driscoll sounded casual, but Liam wasn't fooled. He knew the manager was checking on more than their pitching and catching mechanics; well aware of their past, Coach Driscoll was also checking that they were getting along.

"Everything is great," Liam assured him. Phillip echoed the sentiment.

Coach Driscoll nodded with satisfaction. "I'm glad," he said, "for a lot of reasons. Carry on."

The first game of the Southern California South Sub-Divisionals was set to start. The tournament consisted of two pools, SoCal South and SoCal North, each with five teams. It was a double-elimination format, meaning if a team lost twice, it was out. At the end of pool play, the top SoCal South team would play the top SoCal North team in a best-of-three series. The winner would be the Southern California champion and advance to the Western Regional Tournament.

Before the game, the managers from Ravenna and Wheaton had tossed a coin to determine which would be the home team. Wheaton won. So when the game began, its players jogged out onto the field.

In the dugout behind third base, Mr. Madding, Ravenna's assistant coach, barked out the batting order. "Blackburn! DiMaggio! Finch!"

Shortstop Dominic Blackburn was already wearing a protective helmet over his hair. Now he selected a bat and headed toward the plate.

"Watch your step, Dom!" Rodney yelled to his teammate. Laughter rippled through the players on the bench.

Dom, like many ballplayers, was a fervent believer in the power of superstitious rituals. Before every game, he ate the same "lucky" snack—apple slices with peanut butter—and listened to the same "lucky" song. He believed that it was bad luck to step on the foul line when heading toward the batter's box. When playing defense, he tried to throw the "whammy" on the other team's batters by touching the Little League patch on his left sleeve before every pitch.

Grinning, Dom hopped nimbly over the chalk foul line, sending a new wave of laughter down the bench.

"You believe in superstitions like that?" Liam asked Rodney.

Rodney puffed out his chest. "The only thing I believe in is being awesome," he said with mock bravado, then added, "although I do wear the same underwear every game."

Christopher Frost wrinkled his face in disgust. "Tell me you change them between games when we play a doubleheader. Please!"

"If it makes you feel better, then yes," Rodney said solemnly, "I absolutely change them between games."

Chris peered at him through his glasses and then shifted a few inches away from the right fielder, making his teammates laugh again.

Crack! The laughter turned to cheers as Dom walloped the ball for a single. Phillip followed that hit with an attempted bunt. He missed for strike one. Coach Driscoll signaled for him to swing away. Phillip did and connected for a weak grounder. The Wheaton pitcher fielded the ball cleanly and underhanded it to first base. Phillip was out—and so was Dom when the ball sailed past him to the player covering second. Matt Finch ended Ravenna's chances of getting on the board that inning by popping out to center field.

Liam stood up to put on his catcher's gear. Rodney helped him with the chest protector. "So do you have any rituals or superstitious stuff?" the outfielder asked.

Liam thought for a moment and then shrugged. "Sort of. When I lived in Pennsylvania, Carter and I would fist-bump three times for luck." He smiled. "Actually, we still do that when we video-chat. It's kind of a special thing between the two of us."

He turned to grab his mitt and caught Phillip staring at him. "Everything okay?" Liam asked.

"Um, yeah," the pitcher replied. "It's just, I remember you—"

"Let's go, boys," Coach Driscoll called. "The umpire's waiting."

Whatever Phillip was about to say was left in the dugout as he hurried onto the field.

Liam suited up his catcher's gear, trundled out to home plate, and assumed his crouch. His heart hammered in his chest but not with nerves. He was excited, ready, and raring to go.

Bat in hand, Wheaton's leadoff hitter trotted out of the first-base dugout and stepped into the batter's box.

"Play ball!" the umpire called.

Here we go, Liam thought. He flashed the signal for a fastball, high and outside. Phillip gave a curt nod and then went into his windup. His pitch was powerful and thrown to the exact spot Liam had signaled for. The batter swung and missed.

The umpire raised his arm and showed a clenched fist to indicate a strike. Phillip threw two more pitches. The umpire repeated his strike motion twice more.

"One up, one down, two outs to go," Liam said to himself as the Wheaton batter returned to the dugout amid a smattering of encouraging applause from his teammates.

The second hitter watched the first pitch sail into Liam's mitt. He lined the next between first and second. The ball struck the base path dirt before bouncing into the outfield. Rodney was already racing in.

But as he bent down to scoop the ball into his glove, he tripped—and flipped over in a somersault! Somehow he landed on his feet, but the unexpected forward roll had left him off balance. The runner reached first safe and sound.

One sacrifice bunt later, that same runner was at second. He didn't reach home, however. The fourth batter in Wheaton's order popped out to end the inning.

Rodney was up first for Ravenna. "Time to be awesome," Liam called to his friend.

Rodney responded with a sizzling liner to the left of the mound. Wheaton's pitcher made a valiant attempt to nab the ball in the air but missed. The ball landed between short and second. The Wheaton shortstop snared it as Rodney raced to first.

"Go, Rodney, go!" Liam and his teammates yelled.

Ball hit glove a second after Rodney touched the bag.

"Safe!" the umpire called.

"Awesome!" the boys in the Ravenna dugout cheered.

Liam was up next. He glanced at Coach Driscoll to see if he should bunt. The coach kept his arms at his sides. Liam stepped into the batter's box, ready to hit away.

"Move back! Move back!" the Wheaton catcher bellowed to his outfielders.

The warning was music to Liam's ears. *He's worried I'll wallop it behind them!*

In the end, it didn't matter where the outfielders stood. Liam sent the ball where no one could get it— over the fence for a home run!

CHAPTER

Carter and Ash drove separately to the Pennsylvania State Tournament site. Carter was grateful to have the backseat of his parents' sedan to himself. As much as he liked Ash, sometimes he welcomed a break from the catcher's intensity.

During the hour-long ride, he thumbed through a small book one of his good friends and former teammates had made for him. Rachel Warburton had been a last-minute addition to the Hawks roster. A few of the boys had been a little leery of having a girl on the team. But her easy smile, quirky sense of humor, and strong baseball skills soon won them over—even Ash, who had been the most concerned with her presence.

Carter had always liked Rachel, in part because she reminded him of Liam. Like his cousin, Rachel recognized that Carter pitched better when he was relaxed. So she told stupid jokes or acted a little bit goofy in the dugout to make him laugh. And she reminded him that baseball was a game and that games are meant to be fun, not stressful.

As Rachel had once said, "We *play* games; we don't *work* them."

Rachel wasn't on the All-Star team, but she was still making him laugh thanks to the book she'd made for him. The pages were filled with lame jokes accompanied by silly illustrations she'd drawn. He kept the book in his equipment bag and stole peeks at it during games whenever he felt the pressure mounting.

"Hey, Carter," his mother said, turning around from the passenger seat to smile at him, "looks like we made it!"

"Just in time, too," Mr. Jones added. "I think it's going to start raining any second. Keep an eye out for your dormitory, okay?"

Carter sat up straighter and looked out the car window. He had never been to this university campus before. The previous year's State tournament had been at a different location. As they passed big brick buildings, he tried to read the names etched in stone above their doorways.

He had just spotted his dorm when the first fat raindrops struck the windshield. "Right here, Dad," he cried.

Mr. Jones cut the wheel and pulled up to a small two-story structure. He grabbed Carter's stuff out of the trunk, and they hurried inside.

A cheerful woman holding a tablet computer met them at the door. "Welcome! I'm Mrs. Fullerton, Forest Park's tournament hostess. You have any questions, just ask me," she said. "And you are?"

"Carter Jones."

Nodding, she moved her finger around the touch screen. "You're in room 212. This way!"

She led Carter and his parents up a flight of stairs and down a hallway. "Lucky you, your roomie isn't here yet," she observed as she opened the door. "That means you get to choose which bed you want." Mrs. Fullerton pointed out the way to the bathroom, told him there was a recreation room in the basement, reminded him that the player banquet started at six o'clock sharp, and then left.

Mr. Jones sat on one of the twin beds. "Not bad," he said, bouncing on it a bit. "Maybe I'll stay here instead of our bed-and-breakfast."

Carter grinned. "Sorry, Dad. Players only!"

Mr. Jones stood up, pretending to be hurt. "Hmph. I know when I'm not wanted. Come on, dear."

Mrs. Jones gave Carter a quick peck on the cheek. Then she and her husband departed, shutting the door behind them with a soft click.

Carter tossed his pillow and duffel bag onto the bed. He could hear muffled thuds, music, and laughter coming from nearby rooms. He knew that his teammates were the ones making the noise and that he ought to let them know he'd arrived. Instead, he decided to try Liam again.

Before he could dial, however, someone called him. *Charlie M.*, the caller ID reported.

"Yo, get out here!" Forest Park's outfielder cried when Carter answered. "It's time to play."

Carter was startled. "But the tourney doesn't start until—"

"Just get out here!" Charlie barked. Then he hung up.

Mystified, Carter opened his door to find Charlie Murray, Charlie Santiago, and Peter Molina waiting for him in the hall. Eyes twinkling with mischief, Charlie M. held out a Ping-Pong paddle. "Like I said, it's time to play. You and me against these two. Let's go!"

Carter laughed and followed the threesome to the dorm rec room. It was a sizable space, with a pool table, comfortable couches in front of a flat-screen television, and an old-fashioned pinball game in one corner, as well as the Ping-Pong table. They had the place to themselves now, but Carter was sure it would be overrun with Little Leaguers after the banquet that night.

Thanks to lots of time spent playing Liam in his basement, Carter was a decent Ping-Pong player. Or, at least, he had been. He'd picked up a paddle only a handful of times since Liam moved away.

"I might be a little rusty," he confessed to the others.

His muscles soon remembered what to do, however. He and Charlie M. won the first game. Peter and Charlie S. took the second.

They were midway through a tiebreaking third when Peter suddenly gave a shout. "Holy cow, is that the time?" He pointed at a wall clock behind Carter.

"The banquet's starting in half an hour!" Charlie S. cried.

"Why didn't anyone call us?" Charlie M. pulled his cell phone from his pocket and groaned. "No signal!"

"Maybe it's blocked by these concrete walls," Peter guessed.

"Who cares about that?" Carter said. "We gotta get going or we'll be late!"

They thundered up the two flights of stairs at lightning speed and hurried off to their rooms. Carter threw open the door to number 212—and almost ran smack into Ash.

"Where've you been?" Ash asked, his voice full of exasperation. "I called you, like, twenty times!"

"Sorry, sorry!" Carter tried to explain about the concrete interfering with the signal, but Ash cut him off.

"Just get ready, will you? We're supposed to meet downstairs in five minutes."

As Carter changed into appropriate attire—collared shirt, khaki pants, decent shoes—he checked his phone. Sure enough, the tiny screen reported several missed calls. Five were from Ash. A sixth, he saw with frustration, was from Liam, who had also texted him.

Yo, dork! the message read. *We won! Call later.*

Carter wanted to call then and there, but he didn't. Or rather, he couldn't, because at that moment his phone signaled that its battery was low. "Rats," he muttered as he dug through his belongings.

"Let's go, Carter!" Ash called impatiently from the hallway. "Everybody's waiting for you!"

"On my way!"

Carter found the charger, plugged in his phone, and left to join his teammates for the banquet.

CHAPTER FIVE

After he sent Carter the text about Ravenna's win, Liam gave his phone back to his mother and hurried over to Sean and Rodney. The brothers were goofing around by the bleachers while their father had a brief chat with one of the tournament officials.

"A homer, a single, and a ribbie in three trips to the plate? Man, you were on fire today!" Sean complimented Liam enthusiastically. "Oh, and I guess you did okay, too," he added, giving his brother a playful punch in the gut. "When you weren't doing gymnastics in the outfield, that is."

"Permission to include that somersault in my best-of-Rodney blooper reel?"

The request was from Liam's sister, Melanie, who joined them near the bleachers. As always, she had her video camera with her. She watched most of his games on its small screen as she recorded them, even though— as Liam often pointed out—the action was taking place right in front of her.

Rodney groaned. "Just how many of those bloopers do you have now, anyway?"

"Tons. But there's always room for one more!" Melanie patted her camera contentedly.

"Don't worry," Sean stage-whispered to Rodney, "if you give me ten bucks, I'll swipe it from her next game when she's not looking."

"You do, and I'll swipe you," Melanie warned.

"Yikes! Deal's off, bro!" Sean said, jumping away from Rodney in pretend panic. "I could still use that money, though, for the concession stand tomorrow." He sidled up to Melanie. "I bet I could get some footage of Rodney doing something stupid when we get back home. If I do, want to buy it from me for, say, ten bucks?"

He didn't hear if she wanted to or not—he was too busy running away from his brother.

"The way they act, you'd never know they weren't related by blood," Melanie commented. Then she and Liam cracked up, because anyone who looked at the

Driscoll brothers would see they weren't blood relatives. Rodney was dark-skinned with curly black hair and deep brown eyes. Redheaded Sean was almost the complete opposite: His fair skin was covered with freckles and his eyes were a clear blue. Both had been foster kids until they were seven; that's when Coach Driscoll adopted them.

Liam and Melanie met up with their parents in the parking lot a few minutes later. Mr. and Mrs. McGrath congratulated Liam again heartily and then said they'd like to invite his teammates and their families to their house for a celebratory cookout later that evening. The tournament site was close to their hometown, so pulling together a last-minute gathering wasn't difficult.

"Nothing fancy, though," Mrs. McGrath warned, "just burgers and hot dogs, chips and watermelon!"

That menu worked for everyone, particularly the parents who said they were happy to contribute store-bought items if it meant they wouldn't have to cook.

"See you all later!" Liam called to the other Ravenna players as the McGraths pulled out of the lot. An hour and one hot shower later, Liam was organizing paper goods for the cookout when he realized his cell phone wasn't in his pocket. After a moment of panic, he remembered he'd left it on his bedside table instead of bringing it with him to the ball field. He ran up to his room to get it.

That's when he saw he had missed a call from Carter. He felt a slight pang of guilt. He'd practically hung up on his cousin two days ago and hadn't been in touch since.

He glanced at the clock. It was two thirty. *If I call now, I might catch him before the banquet,* he thought. But Carter didn't answer. So Liam sent a text to tell him that Ravenna had won. Then he stuck the phone into his shorts pocket and returned to the kitchen.

People began to arrive a few hours later; by seven o'clock the backyard bash was in full swing. All the burgers and hot dogs had been eaten, but there was still plenty of food. Everyone had brought something—soda, juice, fruit, cupcakes, and one of Liam's favorite summertime treats: ice-cream sandwiches. Liam was polishing off his second one when he felt his phone vibrate. It was a reply from Carter: *Call me when you get this!*

Liam glanced at the crowd. *I'll only be gone a few minutes,* he thought. *They won't miss me.* But he'd gone only a few steps toward the house when someone called his name.

"Liam!" James Thrasher hurried over to him. He held up a small yellow water balloon for Liam to see.

"Check it out! Cole brought two coolers full of these babies. C'mon, we're choosing sides for a massive battle!"

Liam hesitated. The California sun was still shining bright and hot. Getting soaked by water balloons sounded heavenly.

Then he looked at his phone. "Can you ask the guys to wait, like, five minutes? I just have to make a quick call."

James shrugged. "I'll try, but something tells me this war may start without you."

Liam watched as James went back to the party. Then he stepped inside the house and headed to the kitchen. Looking out the window to the backyard, he saw that the water balloon fight was about to begin. Once it did, he suspected it wouldn't last more than a minute. He sighed. Then he dialed Carter's number.

His cousin picked up on the first ring. "Hey, doofus! Congrats on your win!"

When he heard Carter's voice, Liam grinned. Suddenly, he didn't care about missing the water balloon fight. Some things were more important. He turned away from the window and replied, "Thanks, dork. So what's up?"

Liam didn't know what he expected Carter to say, but it certainly wasn't what he heard.

"I found out something about Phillip."

CHAPTER SIX

The rain had passed and the sun had set during the Pennsylvania State Little League banquet, leaving behind a clear night sky dotted with stars and a crescent moon. Phone pressed to his ear, Carter shifted uncomfortably on the concrete steps outside his dormitory. Above him, moths and other insects battered themselves against the entrance light. Countless others whined and hummed in the distance. To Carter, their sounds seemed amplified by Liam's silence.

"Listen, dork," Liam finally said, "I don't know what you found out about Phillip, but—"

"Just hear me out, will you?" Carter interrupted.

"Fine," Liam replied. "What?"

"Okay, so you know that video Melanie sent me the other day?"

Liam let out an impatient breath. "Yeah, but what does my blooper reel have to do with Phillip?"

Carter blinked in confusion. "Blooper reel?" he echoed. "What blooper—hang on." Realization suddenly dawned on him. "*That's* what you think she sent me? Clips of you being a doofus? Because that is *not* what I got."

"It isn't?"

"No! I got a bunch of footage of Phillip pitching." With that, Carter explained everything. "So I just thought you should know about the face-wipe so you could tell him," he finished.

Liam was quiet for a long moment afterward. "Who else knows about it? Besides Ashley, I mean, because obviously he was there."

"Come on, Liam, call him *Ash.* You know he hates to be called Ashley," Carter admonished. "And besides, you have him to thank. He's the one who saw the 'tell' first."

"Whatever. So are you the only two who saw the video?"

Carter squirmed on the steps again. His discomfort this time came from knowing Liam wasn't going to like his reply.

He had been the last Forest Park player to reach the dorm lobby before the banquet. Mr. Harrison, the team manager, was off to one side, conversing with his assistant coaches, Mr. Filbert and Mr. Walker. His teammates were talking together, too—or rather, they were listening to Ash talk.

"Not just now and then," Carter heard the catcher say, "but *every time*." Then Ash did a perfect imitation of Phillip wiping his face on his shoulder.

Carter didn't say anything then, but he pulled Ash aside as the boys walked to the banquet. "Why'd you tell them about Phillip?" he demanded to know.

Ash gave him a look. "What's the big deal, since you're going to tell Liam anyway? Chances are if we ever face Ravenna, Phillip will have stopped doing it. So..." He shrugged.

Carter figured Ash was right. "Still, I wish you'd let me talk to Liam first," he had muttered.

Now he took a deep breath and told Liam the truth. "No one else *saw* it. But the guys on the team all heard about it."

Liam groaned. "Oh, great, so now—"

Whatever he was going to say was drowned out by a shout of laughter loud enough to travel the phone line from California to Pennsylvania. Then someone yelled, "Dude, c'mon. We need our number one hitter out back!"

When Liam came back, he sounded different. "Hey, yeah, um, listen, I gotta get going, okay? We're hosting a cookout to celebrate Ravenna's win, and someone just came in to find me for a game of Wiffle ball. So catch you later!"

Before Carter could reply, the line went dead.

He hunched forward, elbows on knees, and stared at the CALL ENDED notification on his phone's screen without really seeing it.

Liam hadn't named the "someone," but Carter would have recognized Phillip's voice anywhere. Hearing him say "number one" sent Carter rocketing two years back in time, to Little League Baseball Camp and the humiliation he'd felt every time Phillip had called him Number One Fan. Then he fast-forwarded to the present, to a picture of Liam and Phillip laughing and playing ball together.

For a brief moment, he wished he'd listened to Ash and kept his mouth shut.

It's too late now, he thought, pushing himself up from the steps. *If we do ever meet Ravenna, we'll have to beat them fair and square.*

The sound of Phillip's laughter echoed in his head

as he climbed the stairs to his and Ash's room. *Not beat them,* he amended. *Crush them.*

He went to bed that night with a newfound sense of determination. There was only one place Forest Park could meet Ravenna, and that was at the Little League Baseball World Series. Getting there meant winning States and then Regionals. That journey started the next evening with their first game of States.

He rolled over and looked at the figure in the other bed. "Hey, Ash, you awake?" he whispered.

Ash murmured a sleepy reply. "Sort of. Why?"

"You think we can win tomorrow?"

"Think?" Ash sounded more alert now. He sounded confident, too. "Carter, I don't think we can, I know we can. Because we've got a fantastic team and awesome coaches. And we have something I bet no other team has."

"Yeah? What?"

"A southpaw who throws a killer knuckleball. That pitch of yours is our secret weapon, man. Now go to sleep."

Carter smiled in the dark. "Okay. And thanks."

"Shhhh," Ash replied. "I'm sleeping."

The Pennsylvania State Tournament started the next day. The eight teams competing were divided into two pools, four in East and four in West. Unlike the Southern California Tournament, it was not a double-elimination format. Rather, each team played the others in its pool. After pool play, the top two teams in each pool advanced to the semifinals. The semifinal winners faced each other in a deciding championship game. The victors of that game were crowned the State champs and moved on to the Mid-Atlantic Regional Tournament held in Bristol, Connecticut.

Forest Park was in the West pool and scheduled to play its first game at seven that evening. That left the players free to relax in their dorms or with their families, swim in the university's Olympic-size pool, or watch the other two games being played earlier in the day. Most of them chose to attend the games.

"Gotta check out the competition," Ash said as the players made their way into the stands.

"Yeah," Charlie S. agreed. "By the way, where's your famous binder?"

Ash took his role as catcher very seriously. Part of his duties, he believed, was to maintain scouting reports on every player of every team Forest Park might face. He kept those reports in a blue three-ring binder that he carried with him at all times. Seeing him without it now raised many eyebrows.

Ash made a face. "You know that huge puddle outside our dorm? I dropped my binder in it when I was running to get out of the rain yesterday afternoon. The pages are currently spread around my mom's hotel room, drying out. Not that I'll be able to read them," he added, shaking his head morosely. "The ink ran, and everything I wrote is one big smudge. Two years' worth of scouting, *pfft*, down the drain."

Charlie S. patted his arm sympathetically. "Guess you'll just have to rely on your instincts and reactions, like the rest of us."

Ash rolled his eyes. "Like that makes me feel better?"

Charlie turned his pat into a shove and laughed.

Ash laughed, too. "Ah, no worries, right?" he said. He elbowed Carter in the ribs. "After all, this guy's on the mound today. I don't need any notes to remember what happens when he pitches!"

"Yeah," the other players agreed enthusiastically. "We win!"

Carter joined in the laughter that followed. But deep inside, he felt a twinge of anxiety. *They all expect you to win*, a little voice said. *But what if you don't?*

CHAPTER

SEVEN

Hey, Phillip, how's it going?" When Liam caught up to the pitcher outside the ball fields Sunday morning, he had an eerie feeling of déjà vu, for once again he had something important he needed to say to Phillip.

This time, though, he didn't know quite *how* to say it.

After he'd hung up with Carter the night before, he'd gone out to play Wiffle ball with his teammates. When the last guest departed, though, he grabbed Melanie's arm and pulled her into the house.

"Hey, what gives?" she protested. "We're supposed to clean up!"

Liam yelled to their folks that they'd be back out to help. Then he led Melanie to her computer. "Apparently, you sent Carter the wrong video," he growled. "The one he got was a bunch of clips of Phillip pitching. I need to see it."

Melanie's eyes widened. She sat down and began clicking through desktop icons. "I know the one he means." She opened a folder marked PITCHING. "Voilà!"

Liam leaned forward to get a better look at the images moving across the screen. "There!" he cried after a few moments. "Stop it there!"

Melanie hit PAUSE. The video halted on a close-up of Phillip. He was tilting his head to one side, his cheek aimed at his right shoulder. "Can you play it in slow motion?" Liam asked.

Melanie did as he requested. Liam watched as Phillip dragged his cheek across his shoulder and then went into his windup. The camera zoomed out at that point to show all of Phillip. Melanie must have been standing behind the backstop, because when Phillip lunged forward and released the pitch, the ball looked as if it were coming right at them.

"That would be awesome in 3-D," Melanie murmured.

"Stop it again," Liam ordered. "Now, can you back up the video until just before he lets go and then zoom in on his pitching hand?"

A few clicks and finger swipes later, Liam could see how Phillip was gripping the ball.

Phillip had three pitches in his arsenal: the two-seam fastball, the four-seam fastball, and the changeup. The delivery was basically the same for all three, but the grip was different for the changeup. With fastballs, the ball was gripped by the fingertips. With changeups, it was held deeper in the palm. That placement increased the amount of friction on the ball as it was thrown. The more friction, the slower the ball moved, which was why the changeup was also known as an off-speed pitch.

The ball in Phillip's hand was deep in the palm. He was throwing a changeup.

Liam picked out the same pattern four more times. Then he saw something that made him suck in his breath: a clip of him fist-bumping Phillip three times. That fist-bump was his and Carter's good-luck move. He had no recollection of doing it with Phillip. But there it was, plain as day—and if he'd seen it, Carter had, too.

And knowing Carter, Liam thought, *he won't say any-thing about it unless I force him to.* He promised himself that he'd do just that the next time he and Carter talked.

After the video ended, Liam lay on the floor. "Carter

was right," he said, staring at the ceiling. "Phillip has a 'tell.'"

"Like in a bluffing game, when someone is trying to hide something, but they do something that gives it away?" Melanie asked. She answered her own question. "Oh, I see it. Face-wipe and then that whatchamacallit pitch."

She spun in her chair to look at Liam. "Good thing I sent Carter the wrong video, huh?"

Liam stared at her incredulously. "Why would you say that? Now everyone on the Forest Park team knows he does it! What if we face them? What if—"

"Duh!" Melanie jabbed her bare toe into Liam's stomach. "Earth to Liam! What if you told Phillip about it?"

"Oh." Liam shoved her foot aside and sat up. "I hadn't thought of that. I guess I'll talk to him tomorrow before the game."

It wasn't until he was in bed that night that he saw a possible flaw in the plan.

Phillip didn't like being talked about. He *really* didn't like that Liam and Carter talked about him. So how would he react when he found out Carter had discovered his "tell"? Not well, that's how.

It took Liam a while to get to sleep that night.

Luckily, he dozed in the car on the way to the game and woke up feeling more refreshed. And even better, he had woken up with a new plan.

He put that plan in motion when he saw Phillip. After greeting him, he asked, "Would you answer a hypothetical question for me?"

"Sure. What?"

"Say you noticed a pitcher doing this thing on the mound that advertises something important to batters," Liam said. "Would you tell him?"

Phillip gave Liam a knowing sidelong glance. "You're talking about Carter, aren't you?"

Liam stopped dead in his tracks. "Carter?"

"Oh, yeah. The way he hurls the ball into his glove over and over?" Phillip shook his head. "Dead giveaway that he's tense. Tension can lead to lousy pitching. Lousy pitching means balls, not strikes. If I saw him doing this"—he did a perfect imitation of Carter's ball-throwing habit—"then you better believe I'm going to let the first pitch go by."

Liam was dumbstruck. But after making a mental note to suggest to Carter that he stop his ball-hurling habit, he quickly pulled himself together. "Um, listen, that may be true—and I'm not saying it is—but he's not the guy I'm talking about. You are."

Now it was Phillip's turn to stop in surprise. "Me?"

Liam nodded. Then he told him everything, including that Carter was the one who passed along the information about the "tell" in the first place.

Phillip's jaw dropped. "No way! I didn't think anyone would ever notice that!"

Liam blinked. "Wait a minute. Are you saying you do that on purpose? Why?"

"Dom jumps the foul line. You and Carter bump fists three times. I wipe my face on my shoulder before every changeup."

Comprehension flooded Liam's brain. "It's your superstitious ritual," he said.

"Correction," Phillip said, his expression darkening. "It *was* my superstitious ritual. But now that Carter knows about it, I'll have to give it up, won't I?" He turned on his heel and walked away.

Liam watched him for a moment. Then he shook his head. "Nope. Not going through this again." He ran after the pitcher and caught him by the arm. "Listen, how about we come up with a new ritual, something no one would see or know about but me"—he touched his chest—"maybe Coach Driscoll"—and his nose—"and you?" He pointed at Phillip.

For a long moment, Phillip didn't say anything. Then he gave a half smile. "Okay," he said.

"Good. Now come on. We've got a game to play!"

"Correction," Phillip said again. "We've got a game to *win*!"

Ravenna's second game of the tournament was against Fair Valley. Players on each side looked determined to add another check mark in their win column.

Because they had played more than half the game the day before, Liam and Phillip started on the bench this time. They subbed in at the fourth inning: Liam heading to left field and Phillip to third base. Ravenna was up 4–3, but Fair Valley had runners on first and second—and at the plate stood a batter with a reputation for hitting long balls.

Sure enough, the batter clocked a zinger just out of Dom's reach. Liam was already on the move. He couldn't catch the ball before it hit the ground but stopped it after one bounce. He threw to Phillip. Phillip caught the ball seconds before the runner reached base.

As the umpire called the out, Phillip hurled the ball to second. Matt Finch snared it, swept his glove down and onto the sliding runner, and then looked expectantly at the second-base umpire.

"Yer out!" the man yelled.

The Ravenna players and fans whooped and cheered. "That's what I'm talking about!" Sean bellowed.

Two innings later, Ravenna's players jogged off the field with another victory in their pockets.

And that's what I'm talking about! Liam thought happily.

CHAPTER
EIGHT

Okay, boys," Coach Harrison said as he guided the Forest Park players onto the diamond, "you know the procedure. Caps off, stand up straight, and make sure I can hear you!"

The teammates lined up along one side of the field, forest-green caps held against their green-and-white jerseys, and, when prompted, sang the national anthem and then recited the Little League pledge in unison. On the other side of the field, the Pine Ridge players in their bright red shirts with gold lettering did the same. Then the teams filed back to their dugouts.

Forest Park had won the coin toss and elected to be the home team. At the umpire's call, the players trotted out onto the field for a last warm-up.

As Carter made his way to the mound, he mentally reviewed what Coach Harrison had told them about Pine Ridge during a team meeting that afternoon.

"Obviously, they won their Section," he'd said, running a hand through his thick black hair. "But, to put it bluntly, they won by the skin of their teeth. Each game was close, and most were won in their final at bat. So what does that tell you about them?"

The players looked at one another. First baseman Keith O'Donnell raised his hand. "Um, that they don't give up?" he ventured.

Mr. Harrison jabbed a finger at him. "Exactly! They don't give up!" His eyes twinkled. "But neither do we, right?"

"Right!"

Don't give up, Carter thought as he threw a warm-up pitch.

The game started a few minutes later. Three batters came up to the plate. Eleven pitches later, Carter had struck out each of them.

"Thanks, Carter," second baseman Freddie Detweiler said when they all reached the dugout. "I didn't even have time to sweat!"

"And he hasn't even thrown the you-know-what yet," Ash added. He pointed to his knuckles and gave an exaggerated wink. The other boys murmured their agreement, shooting Carter looks that spoke volumes about their confidence in his special pitch.

The knot in Carter's stomach gave a sharp twist. He had confidence in his knuckleball, too. But he had never pitched to these players before. Who knew what they could do?

One of the assistant coaches seemed to agree.

"It's only the first inning," Mr. Filbert warned. "Plenty of time for runs to be scored." Then he smiled. "Let's make sure we're the ones scoring them, starting with you, Freddie. You're up first. Then Keith, Craig, and Charlie M."

Freddie hopped up, stuck on a batting helmet, grabbed a bat, and headed to the plate. He must have liked the first pitch, because he swung hard. *Ping!* He connected, dropped the bat, and sprinted for first base.

Unfortunately, his hit was a pop-up right to short. The Pine Ridge player just opened his glove and *plop!*— the ball landed right in the pocket.

Keith fared better with a low-flying grounder that evaded the first and second basemen's gloves. He made it safely to first and then reached second on Craig Ruckel's sacrifice bunt.

That brought up Charlie M.

"Here we go, other Charlie, here we go!" Charlie Santiago yelled.

Charlie M. let the first pitch go by. And the second. Both were called strikes. He stepped out of the box, tapped the bat against his cleats, and then stepped back in—and lifted the third pitch into shallow right field. For many batters, that hit would have been a single. But Charlie was faster than most kids. He flew to first, touched the bag, and kept going.

Keith kept going, too, from second to third and then toward home. The spectators jumped to their feet and applauded madly. Players shouted instructions and encouragement.

The Pine Ridge outfielder hurled the ball to the cut-off man, who spun and threw it to the catcher. Keith hit the dirt and slid feetfirst toward the plate.

Carter held his breath. Keith had had trouble timing his slides. Coach Harrison had been working with him on it, though, so maybe this time—

"Good! Good!" Coach Harrison cried, grinning broadly. Then he and everyone else quieted, waiting for the call.

They didn't have to wait long.

"Safe!" the umpire bellowed, fanning his arms out to either side.

The Forest Park bench erupted in cheers. Keith got up and trotted toward his teammates, his expression nonchalant—until he entered the dugout. Then a huge smile broke across his face. "I did it!" he whooped.

"Well done, Keith, well done," Coach Harrison praised.

"My turn," Ash said. He chose a bat and hustled to the plate. But his turn, and Forest Park's chance to add to the score, ended after just one pitch. He hit a weak grounder and was put out at first.

Carter murmured his sympathy as he helped Ash with his catcher's gear. Ash shrugged. "I'll get one next time," he said. "Now let's focus on picking their guys apart!"

They headed out onto the field. Carter sized up the first Pine Ridge batter. The boy was a lefty, like Carter, and of average build with a bit of black hair showing from beneath his batting helmet. *He doesn't look too intimidating,* he thought. *Still, he's batting cleanup, so better be careful.*

He was glad when Ash signaled for a knuckleball. He scrunched up his hand so the tips of his index and middle fingers were touching the ball's seam. He went through his windup, releasing the ball with as little spin as possible.

It was a near-perfect delivery; the ball practically fluttered as it headed toward the plate. Carter let out the breath he'd been holding.

And then sucked it back in sharply.

Pow! The batter connected. The ball soared into the air as if shot from a cannon. The outfielders raced back, then slowed and watched as the ball dropped behind the fence.

The batter's teammates went wild as he trotted around the bases. A man in the stands pumped his fist in the air and cried, "That's my boy!"

On the mound, Carter started throwing the ball into his glove. Over and over, and with so much force that his palm stung.

Next time, he vowed as he followed the boy into the dugout with his eyes. *I'll get it next time.*

CHAPTER NINE

Rodney shot Liam a look of sympathy. "Oh, man, that's lousy," he said. "Will he let it get to him, do you think?"

Liam, Rodney, and Sean were seated at the Driscolls' kitchen island. They were sharing a pepperoni pizza Coach Driscoll had bought them, ignoring a garden salad he had made them, and streaming Carter's game live on Sean's computer. They groaned as one when they saw the Pine Ridge cleanup batter clock his home run.

Liam tossed a half-eaten slice onto his plate. He'd lost his appetite after seeing the telltale crack of the bat. "I sure hope not," he said in reply to Rodney's question. "But I don't know. It's gotta be pretty devastating to give up a homer with your first pitch at the start of an inning."

He knew if he were there, he'd be doing everything he could to reassure Carter that one run, even a homer, wasn't the end of the world. He hoped Ash was doing the same.

"Okay, Carter, here you go," Liam murmured.

An image of his cousin flashed on the screen. Carter stood on the mound, his green eyes narrowed at the batter, sandy hair stuck to his forehead under his cap. He leaned in. The ball was hidden behind his back, but Liam knew he was twirling it in his hand as he waited for the signal.

"You can do it."

The boys watched and then broke into cheers when Carter fanned the batter on three straight pitches. The next two Pine Ridge players didn't get on base, either.

As the broadcast cut to a commercial, Sean opened the pizza box, noted it was empty, and let the lid fall. "You going to finish that?" he asked, indicating the remains of the slice on Liam's plate.

Liam pushed it toward him. Sean carefully separated the edge with Liam's teeth marks from the rest of the wedge and then began to eat.

"What?" he said when Liam and Rodney exchanged amused glances. "I'm still hungry!"

"Yeah," said Rodney, "your day was pretty tough, what with all that sitting in the stands and eating hot dogs and ice cream and all." He pointed to ketchup and chocolate stains on his brother's shirt.

Sean patted his stomach. "Just doing my part to support the local concession stand."

"Shhhh!" Liam shushed. "The game's back on."

"Now batting for Forest Park...Carter Jones," the broadcaster announced.

"C'mon, c'mon, c'mon, c'mon—YES!" Liam's muttered encouragement turned into a shout when Carter hit a sizzling line drive and reached first. "That's the way!"

Unfortunately, Forest Park's next batters, Raj Turner, Allen Avery, and Charlie Santiago, failed to follow up with hits of their own. The teams switched sides with the score still tied at one. In fact, it stayed that way through the next three innings. Liam was disappointed for Forest Park but psyched that when Pine Ridge's home run hitter got up again in the fourth, Carter struck him out. He imagined Carter was even more psyched.

"Okay, they just have to hold them and then get on the board their last at bat," Rodney commented as

Forest Park took to the field for the sixth inning. "Is Carter still pitching?"

The announcer confirmed that he was. "Jones is now at fifty-one pitches. For those who don't know the Little League rules, if he reaches a count of sixty-six total, he won't be eligible to take the mound again for four days. I sure have enjoyed watching this boy pitch."

Liam whooped. "You got that right!" he cried happily. "Man, I wish he could have heard that!"

"Wish who could have heard what?" a new voice inquired.

Startled, Liam turned to the door. He had been so engrossed in the game he hadn't heard Phillip enter. And Liam judged by Sean's and Rodney's surprised expressions that they hadn't, either.

"I was riding my bike by your house when I saw your dad out front trimming the hedges. He let me in," Phillip explained. He slid onto a stool next to Liam, plucked a cucumber slice out of the salad, and jerked his chin at the computer. "What're you guys watching?"

He got his answer when the announcer boomed, "And Carter Jones strikes out Horace Brenner with his knuckleball!"

Phillip froze, the cucumber in his hand midway to

his mouth. Liam stared at the countertop, unsure of what to do or say. Sean and Rodney shifted uncomfortably on their stools.

Then Phillip popped the veggie into his mouth and said, "So your cousin learned how to throw a knuckleball this year, huh?"

Liam didn't trust his voice, so he just nodded.

Phillip selected a bit of carrot and held it up as if inspecting it. "His catcher have any trouble with it?"

Liam shrugged. He knew, as Phillip obviously did, that the knuckleball could be as difficult to catch as to hit. He knew from experience, too: He had tried catching it a few times in June, when Carter and his mother had paid the McGraths a surprise visit. "I guess not," he said, "since Carter keeps throwing it."

Phillip didn't say anything more, just popped the carrot into his mouth. Liam figured he'd leave now that he knew what they were watching. But the pitcher stayed put, eating bits of vegetables out of the salad one after another.

"Hey, guys," Rodney said, "that Pine Ridge slugger is at bat again." He tapped the computer keyboard to raise the volume.

"Now approaching the plate...Jonathan Boyd. Boyd

has been up twice this game. He hit a home run in the second inning and struck out in the fourth."

"Strike him out again, Carter!" Sean cried.

Liam wanted to add his voice to Sean's, but he didn't, not with Phillip sitting right there.

The kitchen went quiet except for the announcer's voice coming through the laptop speakers.

"Jones looks in. Takes the signal. Now he's going into his windup."

Liam stole a quick glance at Phillip. The pitcher's expression was intent, his eyes glued to the screen.

C'mon, Liam urged his cousin silently, *you got this!*

CHAPTER TEN

*D*on't give up.

That was the thought going through Carter's mind as he wiped the sweat from his brow. The sun was low on the horizon, but the humidity had rolled in along with shadowy clouds that blocked out the stars and moon. The air felt leaden and thick with moisture. Carter did his best to ignore it and focus instead on the batter at the plate.

Just two outs to go, he reminded himself. *Let's make this guy number one.*

The Pine Ridge hitter stood outside the box, adjusting his batting gloves and helmet. Then he stepped in, hefted the bat over his left shoulder, and got into his stance.

Ash flashed the signal: fastball, low and inside. Carter nodded once, went into his windup, and threw. He knew the pitch was off even before the call.

"Ball!"

His teammates yelled encouragement and then quieted as Ash returned the ball and Carter readied himself for the next pitch.

This time, the signal was for a changeup. And this time, Carter's aim was true.

"Strike one!" the umpire yelled. The batter hadn't even tried for it.

He didn't try for the next changeup, either, and with good reason. It missed the strike zone by a few inches.

"Ball two!"

Carter took a deep breath in through his nose and let it out slowly through his mouth. Then he waited for Ash's next signal. When it came, he blinked in consternation.

Knuckleball? But he creamed one of those out of the park!

He chewed his lip, wondering if he should shake off the sign. But he didn't.

It's a killer pitch, he told himself. *You've struck out tons of guys with it. Maybe he just got lucky last time.*

If so, the batter got lucky again.

Pow! The ball sailed so high and so deep it looked as

if it might cut a slit in the darkening clouds overhead. Deafening roars sounded from the Pine Ridge players and their fans as the slugger once again took a home run trot around the bases.

Carter hung his head and wished the ground would open up and swallow him right then and there.

"Hey!" Ash jogged to the mound. Concern was etched across his face. "You okay?"

Carter's lips twisted as he struggled to keep his emotions in check. "I blew it," he finally said.

Ash put a hand on his shoulder. "Listen to me," he said urgently. "You didn't blow it. I did." He shook his head. "I should have had you stick to changeups and fastballs. But we don't have time now to debate about who should have done what. We have to get those last outs and then add runs of our own. Okay?"

Carter took another deep breath. "Okay. Okay, I'm ready."

Ash gave him a thumbs-up and trundled back to the plate.

Carter swallowed hard. *Don't give up.* This time, though, the words didn't motivate him. The next two batters both connected. Fortunately, his teammates stopped them from getting on base. The inning ended with just the one run added to Pine Ridge's side of the board.

Three outs later, that's how the board still looked: Pine Ridge 2, Forest Park 1.

Two hours later Carter lay in his bed in the dark, listening to rain patter against the dorm room window. He was alone because Ash was having a late-night snack with their teammates in the rec room. He had wanted Carter to come, too, but didn't push when Carter said he wasn't hungry.

Carter was about to get up to change into his pajamas when he heard a familiar sound coming from his laptop. The sound meant someone was trying to get in touch with him to video-chat. He glanced at the caller ID and saw it was his mother.

He hadn't spent a lot of time with his parents after the game, preferring to get back to the solitude of his room. But now he was happy to see her, even if it was just on a computer screen.

"Hey, sweetie," she said, her soft voice and warm gaze enveloping him like a well-loved blanket. "You doing okay?"

Carter lifted his shoulders and let them drop. "Not really. After all, it was my fault we lost."

Mrs. Jones's eyebrows lifted. "Huh. That's funny. I could have sworn there were other players on that field today besides you."

"Yeah, I know, but—"

"But nothing. Carter, answer me this: Did you play your best today?"

Carter nodded slowly.

"And do you believe your teammates played their best, too?"

"Coach Harrison said they did, that we all did really well."

"And you should believe him," his mother said. "Everyone watching from the stands does."

Mr. Jones suddenly appeared behind his wife. "She's right. You all played top-notch ball out there. But the hard truth is, sometimes even great teams get beat. That's what happened to Forest Park today. What happens tomorrow"—he shrugged—"well, you can either let today's loss bring you down or use it to bolster your determination. Which is it going to be?"

Carter smiled for the first time since getting to his room. "Hmmm, tough choice, Dad. But I guess I'll choose the second thing."

"Good. Now you two end this call, okay? Your mother is exhausted from all her cheering."

Carter laughed. "You got it. Thanks, Dad."

"See you tomorrow, son."

Carter's mother blew him a kiss good night and then signed off. A moment later, however, the computer signaled that another video call was coming in. Assuming his parents had something more to say, Carter answered without looking at the caller ID. So he was surprised when Liam's face filled the screen.

"Yo, dork." Liam's greeting was subdued. "I watched your game on the computer today."

"Oh. So you already know what happened."

Liam nodded. "It really rots, man. I know you'll win the rest, though."

Carter thought his cousin was about to add something else about the game. But he must have been wrong because all Liam said was, "Well, it must be pretty late there, so I'll let you go. Good luck tomorrow, dork."

"Yeah, you, too."

It was only after he'd signed off that Carter realized they hadn't shared their usual good-luck fist-bump.

CHAPTER ELEVEN

*C*oward. That was Liam's opinion of himself after his brief video-chat with Carter. *You didn't say anything about your talk with Phillip, or about the fist-bump you did with him, or how Phillip listened to Carter's game with you. If that's not cowardly, I don't know what is.*

He was still silently berating himself when he got into bed that night. The only way he could turn off the accusations was to promise his conscience that he'd tell Carter everything the next time they talked.

Monday morning dawned bright and sunny without a hint of humidity. Liam woke up feeling better about holding off talking to Carter.

It would have just brought him down.

After breakfast, he, his parents, and Melanie piled into the car and headed off to the ball fields. Liam couldn't wait to get there. He was playing outfield in Ravenna's game against Zaragoza. Zaragoza had won its first game, beating Desert Rock 7–5. Liam hoped that win was a fluke because he really wanted Ravenna to stay undefeated.

It did. While Zaragoza's players made several strong defensive plays, they also made a lot of errors. Their batting just couldn't compensate for those mistakes. Ravenna, meanwhile, played like a well-oiled machine, with every player contributing something to the winning effort. Final score: Ravenna 9, Zaragoza 2.

The victory gave Ravenna a record of three wins and no losses. It also gave the team a day off on Tuesday while Zaragoza and Fair Valley battled for the right to face Liam and his teammates in the tournament's final game on Wednesday. As much as Liam loved playing ball, he welcomed the day off.

After Monday's win over Zaragoza, Liam had planned to tune in to Carter's game, but Melanie cornered him and Phillip outside the dugout.

"Okay, you two," she said. "You promised me a joint interview last week. I know you're not playing tomorrow, so how about we take care of it this afternoon?" She put her hands on her hips and tossed her long brown hair over her shoulder, staring as if daring them to object.

Liam shook his head in defeat. "She's not going to take no for an answer," he warned Phillip. "Better to just get it over with."

Phillip agreed, and they set the interview for four thirty.

The next day, even though Phillip had promised he'd be there, Liam was a little anxious. When Melanie had arranged this joint interview before, Phillip didn't show up because he had been mad at Liam for talking to Carter. Liam found himself watching the clock as the interview time drew near.

He didn't have to worry. The doorbell rang precisely at four thirty. Liam led Phillip to the living room, where Melanie had her camera set up.

"Let's just jump right into it," she said. "Liam, you and Phillip were once rivals. Now you're teammates. Tell me what it's been like making that transition."

Liam started to reply. Phillip cut him off. "Can I answer that instead?"

Melanie looked surprised but nodded.

"So here's the thing," Phillip said. "Liam and I got off to a rocky start back at the Little League Baseball

World Series. I'm not going to go into what happened there, though, because it's all in the past.

"Instead, I want to tell you how Liam has helped me since then."

Now it was Liam's turn to look surprised.

Phillip grinned. "It's true! You know what I did when I heard you were in California and on a team in my Little League? I started practicing harder and with more focus than I ever had before, because I knew that when we faced each other during the regular season, you'd be gunning for me." His grin broadened. "And I was right, too."

Liam gave a little laugh. "Yeah, you were. And I was practicing, too, for that same reason. Man, I wanted to get a hit off you so badly, I could taste it!"

"And I wanted to strike you out again to prove to myself that that strikeout was no fluke." Phillip shrugged. "By making that my goal, I got better."

"Me too," Liam said.

"And then you became teammates," Melanie prompted. "What was that like?"

"Weird," the boys said in unison. Then they laughed.

"I knew things would be tense," Liam said. "Heck, I thought my stomach was going to flip out of me when I got to that first practice, I was so nervous."

"You didn't show it," Phillip said. "The way you marched up to me and congratulated me on winning the Little League Baseball World Series? You looked totally confident."

"So it was smooth sailing from there on out?" Melanie asked.

"Um, not quite." Liam glanced at Phillip. An unspoken agreement to stay silent about their conflicts passed between them. "But, like, the Little League Baseball World Series stuff, that's all in the past now."

"And what about Carter Jones?" Melanie prodded. "Is he in the past now, too?"

Liam narrowed his eyes. He didn't care for the direction this conversation was heading. But once again, Phillip stepped in.

"Carter and I have had some issues," he said evenly. "But I respect him. He's a really good pitcher. He'd have to be, I guess, to learn how to throw a knuckleball. I mean, I couldn't do it."

Liam turned to him in amazement. "Wait, you tried to learn the knuckleball?"

Phillip nodded. "Tried. Failed. Gave up, actually."

Liam burst out laughing. "Good thing, considering I'm your catcher now. See, I tried to catch Carter's knuckleball. Tried. Failed. Gave up, actually."

"One last question, boys, if you don't mind." Melanie waited for their nods before continuing. "Tell me, what do you think Ravenna's chances are for the postseason?"

"Good," Phillip replied immediately. "Better than good. Really, really good. I mean, we haven't won Sectionals yet, but I think we can. And I think we'll do well at Regionals, too."

"I agree," Liam put in. "In fact, I'd like to make a prediction." He turned and looked directly at the camera. "I predict that with Phillip on the mound, me behind the plate, and all the other guys—Rodney, James, Matt, Dom, Luis, Christopher, Nate, Elton, Carmen, Mason, Cole, heck, even Owen, although he's injured—I predict that together we will go all the way to Williamsport and come home as champions!"

Melanie smiled and turned the camera on herself. "You heard it here first, folks. Stay tuned to see if Liam's bold prediction comes true—or if Ravenna watches the Little League Baseball World Series from California."

CHAPTER
TWELVE

One win, one loss. That was Forest Park's record after its victory over Spotsville on Monday evening. The team hadn't won by a lot, earning just three runs. But since it prevented Spotsville from getting even one, those three were enough.

"A day off," Ash said, stretching luxuriously in his twin bed Tuesday morning. Three games were on the tournament schedule, but Forest Park wasn't in any of them. "I think I'll sleep in!"

He was up ten minutes later.

"Curse my stomach," he grumbled. "It insists on being fed at exactly seven thirty every morning."

Carter was hungry, too, so he got up, dressed, and

joined Ash in the university dining hall for breakfast. Many of their teammates showed up as well, lured, no doubt, by the promise of pancakes, scrambled eggs, bacon, and more. They commandeered their usual table. Players from other teams did the same.

Carter polished off a plate of pancakes and then got up to refill his juice from the big dispenser at the side of the room.

"My older sister throws a mean knuckleball."

Carter spun around to find himself face-to-face with Jonathan Boyd.

"That's how I knew how to hit yours," the Pine Ridge player continued. "She threw it to me in the backyard all regular season. I never thought I'd have to face one. Turns out I was wrong."

"Yeah," was all Carter could think to reply. "Guess so."

Jonathan cocked his head to one side. "No hard feelings, though, right? I mean, we're all doing what we can do to win."

Carter looked away. "The thing is, you never thought you'd face someone who could throw a knuckleball. I never thought I'd face someone who could hit it. At least, not as hard as you did."

"I'm pretty proud of those homers." Jonathan's tone was matter-of-fact, not smug. Then his expression dimmed. "I wish I could have hit one yesterday, too. We needed it."

Pine Ridge had lost its second game, falling to Burton 13–6.

"You're not out of it yet," Carter reminded him. "If you beat Spotsville, you'll be two-and-one for the tournament."

"True, and if you guys beat Burton, you'll have the same record. Good luck with that, though. Those guys can *hit*. Anyway, see you around."

Carter was about to return to his table when he spotted something under Jonathan's arm. "Hey, is that a pin-trading bag?"

Jonathan held open the bag. "Sure is. I go to the Little League Baseball World Series every year to trade. Well, and watch baseball, of course. Do you collect, too?"

"You bet! Wanna meet up after breakfast and do some trading? If no one's using the Ping-Pong table in our rec room, we could meet there."

Jonathan agreed enthusiastically and the two parted.

Back at the Ravenna table, Carter was greeted with stares of amazement. "Were you actually talking with that jerk?" Ash demanded to know.

"Yes, and he's not a jerk. He's just a kid, like us."

Carter filled him and the others in on their conversation.

"I knew there had to be an explanation for why he could hit your knuckleball!" Charlie S. crowed. "I mean, that pitch is Forest Park's winning ticket, our ace in the hole, our bird in the hand, our…our…well, you get the point. It's why we've gotten as far as we have in the postseason. Unless you face Boyd again, it should be smooth sailing for us from here on out."

Carter gave a short, self-deprecating laugh. "Yeah, right."

But to his astonishment and dismay, none of the other players disputed what Charlie S. had said. Carter was so taken aback, he didn't know what to say. So, in the end, he said nothing.

Coach Harrison arrived at their table a few moments later. "So," he said, taking a seat between Charlie S. and Allen Avery, "what's the topic of conversation this morning?"

Charlie S. explained what happened. "I was just telling Carter how important his knuckleball is to us winning games," he added.

"Really." Coach Harrison took a long sip of coffee. He didn't say anything else until the players were done with their meals. "Okay, boys, enjoy some relaxation time this morning. Then let's plan to meet in the dorm lobby before the one o'clock game. Oh, and don't worry about clearing your dishes this morning. Just give them to Carter. He'll take them to the conveyor belt."

With that, he handed Carter a plate sticky with syrup.

The boys looked at one another and then at the belt chugging into the kitchen's back room.

"I can help him if—" Allen started to say.

"No, no," the coach interrupted jovially. "He's capable."

Luke Armstrong shrugged, stood up, and put his plate, silverware, and plastic tumbler on top of the empty plate Carter was already holding. As other boys followed suit, the stack of dirty dishes grew until it teetered alarmingly.

"Uh, coach?" Peter Molina said, hesitating with his plate. "I don't think Carter should have to handle it all by himself."

Suddenly, Coach Harrison stood up and exclaimed, "He shouldn't have to handle your plates—and he shouldn't have to shoulder your expectations, either."

He shook his head. "His knuckleball can be a devastating pitch. But expecting that pitch to be the driving force that gets Forest Park through the postseason?

That's as unreasonable as thinking he can get your dishes to the conveyor belt without dropping them."

"Speaking of which...!" Allen and Peter darted forward and grabbed plates from Carter just as the stack started to slide.

"My point is," the coach said, "you boys are a team. You contribute equally to victories and defeats alike. Do I make myself clear?" He looked at each of them in turn, meeting their eyes and nodding back when they nodded. "Okay. Good. Now off you go. My coffee is getting cold."

The players left, murmuring *see you later* and *bye*. Carter simply said, "Thanks."

Carter met up with Jonathan in the rec room an hour later. Players from other teams heard what they were doing and showed up with their collections, too. By lunchtime the Ping-Pong table was surrounded by boys wearing jerseys of all different colors. "It's like a rainbow threw up down here," one boy commented happily.

The rest of Carter's day was spent just as happily, except for one thing. Jonathan's team lost. To his surprise, though, the Pine Ridge slugger didn't seem too down.

"We're not out of it yet," he reminded Carter. "If you

guys lose big to Burton, we still have a shot at claiming second place in our pool because of the runs-allowed ratio."

Carter grinned. "Guess we'll just have to win big instead, then."

Jonathan shook his head. "Good luck. Burton is one of the toughest teams I've ever faced. They can hit, and their guys are crazy fast on the base paths. But who knows? Maybe you guys will do what we couldn't."

CHAPTER
THIRTEEN

After Tuesday's interview, Liam and Phillip brainstormed ideas to change Phillip's superstitious facewipe gesture. But nothing they came up with seemed quite right to the pitcher.

"Maybe it's a mistake to try switching it now," he said when he left a short while later.

"Maybe," Liam said. But he wasn't convinced. Too many people knew about it—people they just might run into if they made it all the way down the road to Williamsport.

Not if, Liam chastised himself. *When.*

It was Melanie who ended up giving him a new idea. She'd been working on her video documentary when she suddenly gave a loud whoop that brought the family running.

"What is it?" Mrs. McGrath cried.

Melanie's face was wreathed in smiles. "I had this concept for a sequence," she explained. "I've been visualizing it for a few days. But we've been so busy going back and forth to the ball fields that I didn't have time to put it together. Until now."

She pressed a key, and a video started playing. Liam and his parents crowded closer to watch.

An image of a calendar showing the month of June appeared on the screen. The fifteenth was circled in red, with the days leading up to it x-ed out.

"All-Star announcement day," Liam murmured.

Melanie nodded. "That's the starting point of the story."

The calendar faded out, replaced by a distant shot of an empty baseball diamond. Liam recognized it as one his regular-season team, the Pythons, had often played on. The field was in perfect condition: the chalk lines bold and white, the sandy base paths free of scuffs, and the grass a brilliant green.

"Nice," Mrs. McGrath murmured. "How'd you get the shot?"

"Climbed up the backstop and hung on for dear life," Melanie answered.

"Not so nice," Mrs. McGrath said.

The image slowly zoomed in on home plate. Two feet wearing baseball cleats appeared in the batter's box. The tip of a bat tapped the plate.

"Whose feet are those?" Mr. McGrath asked.

"Spencer Park's," Melanie said. "He told me he'd be happy to help with the documentary any time."

Liam choked back a laugh. Spencer had been a pitcher on the Pythons; Liam had caught for him many times. He wasn't surprised to hear Spencer had made such an offer. Liam had long suspected he had a crush on his sister.

Words materialized on the plate: PART ONE: THE JOURNEY BEGINS.

"That title is just a placeholder right now," Melanie hastened to say. "I needed something there to see if this effect would work. Watch!"

A hand holding an umpire's plate brush appeared, hovered over the words for a second, and then started sweeping. The words were cleaned off just as dirt and sand would be in real life.

"Hey, that looks pretty cool!" Liam said, impressed despite himself.

"Thanks. Like I said, I pictured it in my head. Then I made it happen."

Liam looked thoughtful. "Huh. Pictured it in your head…"

Melanie waved a hand in front of his face. "Hello? You in there?"

"I am! I think I just got an idea of my own!" Without explaining, Liam rushed to his room, called Phillip, and asked if he could come by.

"Sure, but why?"

"I have something for us to test. See you in ten!"

His mother had to do an errand, so she dropped him off at Phillip's house. As Liam rang the DiMaggios' doorbell, he realized he'd driven by and ridden his bike past Phillip's house before but never actually been inside.

This should be interesting, he thought as he waited for Phillip to answer the door.

What was interesting was that Phillip didn't answer the door. Owen Berg did. For a moment, Liam thought he had the wrong place.

But then Phillip appeared behind Owen.

"Hey, Liam. Come on in. Owen and I were just playing video games." Phillip turned away, clearly expecting the others to follow. Liam tried to but couldn't because Owen stood firmly planted in the doorway, staring at him. Liam waited for him to move so he could enter. After a long moment Owen finally stepped aside just enough for Liam to squeeze past.

"So what's this all about?" Phillip asked.

Liam darted a glance at Owen. He thought his idea had merit but was pretty sure Owen would think it was stupid. But since he couldn't just leave without telling Phillip about it, he forged ahead.

"What if, instead of actually doing your face-wipe ritual, you just imagine you're doing it? I mean, *really* imagine every little detail so that it felt real."

As if on cue, Owen gave a snort, flopped down in an easy chair, and picked up his video game controller. "Oh, brother," he drawled. "That's your plan?"

"No, hang on, IceBerg," Phillip said. "I remember reading about something like that in one of my sports magazines." He moved to a shelf stacked with old issues and started sorting through them. "It's called visualization or mental guidance. Lots of athletes do it. Sprinters and swimmers see themselves winning a race, for example. Basketball players 'see' their shots, that kind of thing. Yeah, here it is."

He pulled out an issue featuring the last Winter Olympics and winged it to Owen. Owen glanced at the cover, shrugged, and kept playing his game.

"If you want any advice on how to do it," Liam said, warming to his subject, "Coach Driscoll is your man. He knows a lot about mind-over-matter stuff. He taught us that relaxation breathing technique. I bet he knows about this, too."

"I'll talk to him later," Phillip said. "But right now I want to head out back and see if it works."

"Let's go!"

Owen dragged himself up from his chair, muttering. "This I gotta see."

Phillip had a pitch back set up in his yard. He found a ball and got into position. Then he hesitated and looked at Liam uncertainly. "What do I do now?"

"Try closing your eyes and picturing what you usually do," Liam suggested.

"Or forget about trying to change what you do," Owen countered, "because changing it now is going to mess you up."

"Maybe not," Liam said, doing his best to keep his voice even.

"Probably so," Owen said. He gave Liam a long look. "And when it does, it'll be your fault."

CHAPTER
FOURTEEN

No way! Carter couldn't believe his eyes when Liam texted him what Owen had said. It was late Tuesday night. Ash was already asleep in the other bed, so the boys were texting instead of talking or video-chatting. *What did u say?*

Nothing, Liam informed him. *P told O to back off.*

Carter experienced a rush of gratitude mixed with jealousy when he read that. He was glad to know that Phillip had stood up for his cousin. But at the same moment, he flashed back to the video clip of Phillip and Liam bumping fists three times. If it had been anyone else but Phillip . . .

He shook his head to clear it. *Good,* he typed, then added, *G2G. Big game 2morrow.*

BOL, Liam responded, meaning *Best of luck.*

U2, Carter replied. Then he turned off his phone. He didn't close his eyes, though. He was afraid he might start picturing Phillip and Liam hanging out together, playing ball, sharing laughs and private jokes...and becoming best friends while he stood on the outside looking in.

"So how's the great Liam McGrath?"

Carter was startled by the sound of Ash's voice coming out of the darkness. "Sorry, did my texting wake you up?"

"I wasn't asleep." Ash rolled onto his side so he was facing Carter's bed. Carter could just make out the shine of his eyes in the dimly moonlit room.

"Oh," Carter said. "Well, to answer your question, Liam's been having a little trouble with one of the guys who used to be—"

"Yeah, you know what? I'm not really interested." Ash blew out a long breath. "To be honest, I think I could live pretty happily never hearing another word about Liam."

Carter had long suspected Ash was jealous of his relationship with his cousin. He'd kept it more or less to himself, however. Carter figured he didn't want to talk about it, so he never brought it up, either. But now it was out there, hanging in the air between them and impossible to ignore.

Still, Carter stayed silent. Not because he wanted to, but because he couldn't think of what to say to ease Ash's jealousy. And then it struck him.

"I feel the same way about Phillip DiMaggio," he said.

"Then why did you tell Liam about his changeup thing?" Ash demanded. "You had the perfect instrument of revenge right in your hands and you chose to—"

"Because it was the right thing to do," Carter interrupted quietly.

After a moment Ash said, "Yeah, I know. And I know it's stupid for me to be so bothered about you and Liam." He pushed himself up to a sitting position and leaned his head back against the wall, eyes on the dark ceiling overhead. "Maybe I'd feel better if I knew the answer to one question."

Carter struggled up to a sitting position, too, but he swung his legs over the side of the bed so he was facing Ash. "I think I know the question," he said.

Ash rolled his head so he was looking at Carter. "You do?"

Carter nodded. "I've been asking myself the same one. You want to know what's going to happen if Forest Park faces Ravenna at the Little League Baseball World Series. What I'll do if I have to play against Liam."

Now Ash twisted around, feet on the floor, so he was facing Carter. He put his elbows on his knees and leaned in close. Even in the near-complete dark, his gaze was intense. "That's *exactly* what I want to know."

Carter looked away, unable to meet that gaze any longer. "I wish I could tell you," he replied. "But the truth is, I don't know myself. I guess I'm just hoping that I'm never in a position where I have to find out."

"That would mean either Forest Park doesn't make it all the way, or Ravenna doesn't."

"I know," Carter said miserably. "The trouble is, as much as I'm dying to get another shot at the Little League Baseball World Series title, I want Liam to get that shot, too. You weren't there last year. You didn't see that strikeout. I wish I could wipe it from my brain."

Ash studied him for a long moment. Then he tucked his legs back under his covers and lay down. "The thing is, Carter, if Forest Park does face Ravenna"—he turned and looked at Carter again—"you may be the one striking him out this year. The sooner you get used to that idea, the better it will be for you and for the team."

Carter put his head in his hands and dug his fingers into his hair. "Yeah," he said. "I know."

It took him a long time to get to sleep that night.

CHAPTER

Undefeated. That's a nice word, isn't it?" Coach Driscoll said to his team. The boys were waiting for the signal to take the field for the game against Zaragoza. "I don't know about you all, but I wouldn't mind ending pool play that way."

The Ravenna players shouted their agreement. A victory that afternoon would earn them a record of 4–0. Zaragoza, with a final record of 2–2, would be eliminated from the tournament. Fair Valley, Wheaton, and Desert Rock had already suffered two losses each and were out.

If Zaragoza won, however, it would be tied with Ravenna at 3–1, forcing the two teams to play a tiebreaker the next day. The winner of that game would move on to play against the top team from Southern California North in the Southern California Championship.

With so much on the line, Liam had expected Phillip to start the game at pitcher—with Liam as his catcher, of course. And Phillip was the team's best pitcher, so starting him made sense.

But when Coach Driscoll tapped Mason Sykes to start, a small part of Liam was relieved.

Yesterday, Phillip hadn't seemed very comfortable throwing a changeup without his face-wipe gesture. Liam didn't give up on the visualization idea, though. Together, they went to the Driscolls' to talk to the coach.

Coach Driscoll encouraged Phillip to keep trying and suggested he watch Melanie's footage to help get a clear picture in his mind of what the face-wipe gesture looked like. Melanie had given Phillip a copy that evening.

"I watched the clips over and over," Phillip had told Liam that morning. "I can see what I do perfectly. Unfortunately, it was too dark out last night for me to try the changeup again."

"Don't worry," Liam said reassuringly. "I'm sure you'll do great."

Deep down, though, he wished Phillip had had time to practice the visualization technique for real at least a few times. So when the game began, he was happy to cheer on his teammates from the bench. But he kept it to himself.

He and Phillip subbed in after the third inning, but not as catcher and pitcher. Instead, Coach Driscoll assigned them to outfield and third base. They both did well there and contributed to the offensive efforts with a single apiece. Neither managed to reach home, though.

Just before the end of Ravenna's at bat, Coach Driscoll called them over.

"Phillip, you're pitching. Liam, suit up in your catcher's gear." He named other players and the positions they'd be assuming that inning. With the score Ravenna 5, Zaragoza 4 at the top of the fifth, he sent them all onto the field with one instruction: "Hold them."

Liam caught Phillip's eye then. On the spur of the moment, he did the nose-bop gesture—but with a modification. Instead of touching his chest, he touched his shoulder. Instead of his nose, he tapped his temple. Only then did he point at Phillip.

Phillip grinned his understanding. Then he headed to the mound, where he did as Coach Driscoll had instructed: He held them at four runs by striking out the first three batters. Four of the missed pitches were changeups—minus the face-wipe.

Unfortunately, Zaragoza's pitching was just as strong in the bottom of the fifth. Ravenna got just one hit. The other three batters struck out.

As Liam tugged on his gear for the top of the sixth, he imagined what a sportscaster might say about the previous inning. *"With a shot at the championship on the line, this game is coming down to a classic pitchers' duel."* He hadn't realized he'd said it out loud until James nudged him and said, "Let's cross our fingers that Phillip wins!"

"I'm crossing my toes, too," Dom put in. "And I'd do my eyes if I thought it'd help!"

Phillip didn't add any more strikeouts to his tally. The first batter popped out to Dom. The second hit a grounder that James fielded and sent to Mason, who was now playing first base. And the last batter ticked a foul ball that rose straight in the air and landed right in the pocket of Liam's mitt.

Final score, after five and a half innings: Ravenna 5, Zaragoza 4.

Immediately after the game, Liam and his teammates lined up by home plate to congratulate the Zaragoza players on a good game. The time-honored ritual gave them a chance to see their competitors up close. Out of respect for their opponents' feelings, they made sure their acknowledgments were short but sincere and to keep their own soaring elation hidden.

Once the hand-slap was finished and the teams apart, however, the players gave voice to their joy, with Rodney Driscoll leading the charge as usual.

"Southern California Championship, here we come!" he crowed in the dugout.

Liam joined in the cheers and then started packing up his gear to head home. He was tired, hot, dusty, and preoccupied by thoughts of the cool shower ahead when he noticed Phillip talking to Owen outside the dugout. They were too far away for Liam to hear what they were saying, but he had no trouble reading Owen's body language.

Owen's hands were jammed into his shorts pockets. His shoulders were hunched. He was kicking at the dirt, raising a dusty cloud around them. He was scowling.

Suddenly aware that he was staring, Liam returned to his gear. But then he heard Phillip call his name. He looked up to find the pitcher beckoning him over. Liam hesitated, for Owen still looked annoyed. Curiosity won out, however.

"Hey, what's up?" he asked.

Phillip prodded Owen. "Go on, man. Tell him."

"Tell me what?"

Owen let out an exasperated sigh and rolled his eyes. "Your idea worked." He glared at Phillip. "There, you happy, DiMadge?"

In response, Phillip threw a playful choke hold around Owen's neck and planted noogies across his skull. "Yeah, I'm happy! I'm really happy! You know why? Because we're going to the SoCal Championship!"

"Ow! Quit it!" Owen protested. But his words carried no weight because he was starting to laugh.

Phillip let him go. "You'll be there to cheer us on this weekend, right, IceBerg?"

Owen nodded. "I'll be there and I'll be cheering for you." He cut his eyes to Liam. Then he put out his hand. "Good luck...McG."

Grinning, Liam clasped Owen's hand and replied, "Thanks...IceBerg."

CHAPTER
SIXTEEN

While Liam and his teammates were celebrating their victory over Zaragoza, Carter and the rest of the Forest Park team were heading to the field at the top of the sixth inning. They were playing Burton, a tough team that had overpowered Pine Ridge and Spotsville, winning those games with scores of 13–6 and 7–2. Coach Harrison had called Burton an offensive powerhouse— so the fact that Forest Park had allowed them just one run in five innings had made him and the assistant coaches very happy.

Of course, everyone in the Forest Park dugout would have been happier still if they had earned runs.

Unfortunately, their side of the scoreboard showed nothing but goose eggs.

Carter grabbed his glove and headed to third base. He would have loved to be on the mound to try his hand at shutting down Burton's offense.

But Coach Harrison had elected to keep Peter in instead. Peter was a strong pitcher—some days. Other days, he seemed to let the pressure get to him. He'd been having a very strong game so far. But now he seemed to be tiring.

He walked the first batter. The second laid down a bunt that catcher Ron Davis fielded and sent to first. The batter was out, but the runner reached second. The next batter fouled off three pitches and then missed the fourth.

"There you go, Peter!" Carter cried. "Let's see you do it again!"

Peter didn't do it again. Instead, he threw a fastball that wasn't very fast—and to Burton's cleanup hitter, a tall boy named Marco Bellini.

Crack!

The ball launched off Marco's bat and headed straight to deep center field. Ash, who was playing outfield, took off at a sprint.

"Go, Ash! Go!" Carter cried. He held his breath,

willing Ash to get under it in time, make the catch, and end Burton's chances of adding to the score. The other Forest Park players were in motion—second baseman Freddie racing to cover first, shortstop Allen moving to second, and first baseman Keith positioning himself in the cutoff spot. All were ready to act if Ash didn't make the catch.

He didn't. The ball missed his outstretched glove and dropped into the dirt.

The runner on second was already rounding third and heading to home plate when Ash picked up the ball.

"Here! Here!" Keith screamed.

Ash straightened, reared back, and hurled the ball with all his might. He had one of the most power-ful arms on the team; as a catcher, he had experience throwing the ball while rising from a crouch. Usually, his throws were dead-on accurate. But if he had been aiming for Luke's glove, he missed by a mile.

Oh, no! Carter groaned inwardly.

The ball soared over Keith's head. If it had had a little more oomph, it might have reached Ron. Instead, it fell short of that mark, landing three feet in front of home plate. Peter dashed forward to get it, but he was too late. The runner slid across home plate seconds before the ball hit Ron's mitt.

"Safe!" the umpire cried.

The next batter popped out to end the inning.

The mood in the Forest Park dugout was somber. Ash wouldn't meet anyone's eyes. Carter's attempt to talk to him earned him a glare.

"I blew it, okay?" Ash growled. "I thought I could throw it to home. I couldn't. And if we don't get on board—"

"—we'll still be in the semifinals."

As one, the players snapped around to look at Coach Harrison. He strode to the front of the dugout and stabbed a finger at his clipboard. "The top two teams from each pool advance to the semifinals. If we lose today, we'll be in a three-way tie with Pine Ridge and Spotsville. According to tournament rules, in such a case, second place is awarded to the team that allowed the fewest runs overall." He indicated his clipboard again. "Unless my calculations are wrong, that's us. But let's not rely on my addition! Let's earn the runs we need to beat Burton! Okay?"

"Okay!" the players shouted.

Unfortunately, their enthusiasm didn't translate into hits. Burton swapped pitchers for the last inning. The new pitcher retired the side in order. Final score: Burton 2, Forest Park 0.

Jonathan Boyd caught up to Carter after the game. "Tough loss," the Pine Ridge player sympathized. "But, hey, at least you guys held them to two runs. That's way better than what we did. Or Spotsville."

"Yeah," Carter replied. "I just hope we don't have to face them again. Or if we do, I hope I'm on the mound. I'd like to see what they can do against my knuckleball."

Jonathan nodded. "You have to beat the East's number one team first. That's Jeremiah. I caught one of their games. They look really good." Then he gave Carter a big smile. "But I think you guys can take 'em. And I think you can win the championship game, too, and get to the Mid-Atlantic Regional Tournament. At least, I hope you will. Know why?"

Carter shrugged. "Why?"

"Because me and my team won't be going. And since we won't, I'd like to know someone on the team that will be there. So when you make it—and note I said *when!*—I hope you'll keep in touch and let me know all about it, okay?"

With that, Jonathan dug out a piece of paper and a stub of a pencil and scribbled a number on it. "That's my cell," he said. "Call or text me anytime."

Carter took the paper, tore off a piece, and jotted down his number for Jonathan to have. The two shook hands, and then Jonathan turned and walked away. Carter lost sight of him in the crowd of spectators.

Mr. and Mrs. Jones appeared by Carter's side a moment later. "Who was that?" his mother asked.

Carter glanced at the scrap of paper in his hand and smiled. "A friend," he said.

CHAPTER
SEVENTEEN

Thursday morning Liam woke to an empty house. A note from his mother informed him that she and his father were both at work—his father was a businessman and his mother designed playground equipment for a new company—and Melanie was having breakfast with a friend.

"Take plenty of water with you," the note said. "See you for dinner. Call if you need anything."

Coach Driscoll had called for a light practice that morning and had arranged to pick Liam up at his house. Ten minutes to ten, Liam heard a horn toot. He grabbed his water bottles and hurried to the garage to get his mitt.

"We're just doing some hitting, fielding, and throwing," he said. "No pitching."

A few Ravenna players were already at the field when they arrived. The rest came within a few minutes. All were in high spirits, still jubilant after their undefeated run through pool play.

"I can't wait to take on Hollyhock!" James said, pounding his fist into his glove. "I wish we were playing tomorrow."

"Saturday will be here soon enough," Coach Driscoll said. "Now everyone but Liam into the field. Liam, you stay here behind the plate. I want to see clean pickups and accurate throws that hit Liam's glove smack in the pocket."

When the players had scattered onto the grass, Mr. Madding, the assistant coach, knocked out some grounders for the infielders. After a few minutes, he switched to fungos. He ended with some high-flying hits to the outfielders. Liam, standing to one side of the plate, caught the incoming throws and then fed the ball back to Mr. Madding.

"Looking good, looking good!" Coach Driscoll called. "Now throw to first after the catch!"

The fielding drill continued with the throws going

to second and third. Then Coach Driscoll called the players in for batting practice.

"I understand your cousin's team made it to the semifinals," he said to Liam while watching Rodney take his turn at the plate. "You planning to listen to the broadcast later?"

"Sure am," Liam said. "They play at seven, so that's four our time. I was going to invite Rodney and Sean over, if that'd be okay with you."

"Since your folks won't be home from work yet, why don't you come to our house instead?" the coach offered, then added in a louder voice, "Anyone who wants to listen to the Pennsylvania State semifinals, be at our place at four! Ice cream will be provided."

Such a loud cheer rose from the players that Liam wasn't surprised when a sizable group showed up at the Driscolls' house that afternoon. He helped set out the bowls and spoons and then helped himself to a generous portion of his favorite ice cream, mint chocolate chip. By then, the coach had found the website broadcasting Carter's game. The announcer's voice boomed out of the state-of-the-art sound bar connected to the coach's laptop.

"Welcome to the second semifinal game of the

Pennsylvania State Little League Tournament! For those just tuning in, earlier today the number one West team, Burton, defeated the number two East team, Edgemere, by a score of fourteen to nine. Now Jeremiah, the top East team, will play the West's second-place Forest Park."

Then he announced the lineups for both teams. Liam was a little disappointed to learn that Carter wasn't pitching. But he figured Coach Harrison was saving him for the championship.

When the game began, there was a smattering of applause from the Ravenna players, most of whom were more interested in their ice cream at that point. That changed, though, as the action unfolded, for as much as they loved sundaes, they loved baseball even more.

Forest Park was in the field first. It prevented Jeremiah from scoring and then got on board first with a pair of runs thanks to a single from Craig Ruckel followed by a homer from Charlie Murray.

"Murray is taking the bases at full speed rather than the usual home run trot," the announcer said, his voice amused.

"That sounds like Charlie," Liam said with a laugh. "I swear, his motto is 'Why walk when you can run?'"

Jeremiah answered with three runs at its next at bat.

But Forest Park jumped right back into the lead with two more runs.

"This is shaping up to be another high-scoring game," the broadcaster announced.

That prediction turned out to be true. Both teams added a run nearly every inning. At the bottom of the sixth, the score was tied at seven each.

The boys in the kitchen fell silent as Luke Armstrong came up to bat. So far, Luke had struck out and popped out.

"Come on, Luke, you can do it," Liam murmured. But Luke grounded out.

Next up was Craig. He'd singled twice. He did again. That brought Charlie M. to the plate.

"Think he'll bunt?" Sean whispered to Liam.

"Doubt it," Liam whispered back. "Coach'll trust him to connect."

Charlie M. did. It wasn't a home run but a solid double that advanced Craig to third.

"Now batting, Ash LaBrie," the announcer informed the listeners.

For the first time ever, Liam found himself rooting for Ash. Then he found himself cringing—as the pitch hit Ash right in the ribs!

"Oh, man, I bet that's gonna leave a mark!" Rodney said. "Think the pitcher did it on purpose?"

"If he did, the umpire would have something to say about it," Coach Driscoll said.

The umpire must have thought it was unintentional, however, for play continued uninterrupted.

"And Carter Jones takes his stance."

Liam's stomach flip-flopped when he heard the broadcaster. "Oh, boy. Oh, boy," he said. "C'mon, dork. You can do this." He closed his eyes and sent his cousin all the positive energy he could.

Crack!

"It's a hit to right field! That ball is soaring! Jeremiah's outfielder is racing to get under it! He's almost there, he's reaching—he missed it!"

The Driscolls' kitchen erupted with cheers.

"Quiet!" Liam demanded.

Silence fell. The only voice was that of the announcer as he tracked Craig's dash for home. "He's giving it all he's got, folks, really churning up that base path! He's hit his slide. And...he beats the throw! Ladies and gentlemen, that's the game! Forest Park wins eight to seven!"

"Yes! Yes! Yes!" Liam shouted, pumping his fist in the air with each cry. "They made it to the championship!"

CHAPTER
EIGHTEEN

The sky over Pennsylvania was a brilliant blue Friday afternoon, the July sun bright—and *hot*. Forest Park was scheduled to play Burton at five thirty. By five, when the players ran onto the field to warm up, the temperature on the field had leveled out at ninety degrees. By 5:01, everyone was slick with sweat.

"Man, this is going to be brutal," Ash said in the dugout afterward. He mopped his brow with his sleeve.

Mr. Walker passed out cups of cool water. "I want to see everybody drinking plenty of water between innings, whether you're thirsty or not," he instructed the players. "We have plenty of cold, wet towels for you to put on your heads and necks, too. And if anyone feels the slightest bit dizzy or anything else unusual, you tell me right away."

Carter and the others nodded. They knew the coach was doing everything in his power to prevent possible heat illness. They took his instructions seriously; a player had fainted the day before because he'd become dehydrated. He was fine now, but no one wanted that to happen to him.

Coach Harrison called for the team's attention. "Let's review what we know about Burton. One: They can hit. Their high scores prove that. Two: They are fast on the base paths. I'm talking Charlie Murray fast."

Carter glanced at Charlie M. and grinned. Charlie grinned back, looking a little embarrassed but a lot pleased at the coach's compliment.

"And three," the coach continued, "we came the closest to beating them of any team they've faced in this tournament so far. I believe that if each and every one of you brings his A game today, we can walk away with the win. What do you think?"

The players cheered lustily. A few swung their wet towels in the air.

"Okay! We're the home team, so take one last drink and get on out there."

While the players gathered their gloves, the coach

beckoned to Carter. "I wanted to pass along a compliment from the Pine Ridge manager. He told me that in all his years of coaching Little League, he has never seen a pitcher with as natural a delivery as yours. And I told him that I couldn't agree more."

Carter smiled, certain he was wearing the same expression of pleasure mixed with embarrassment that Charlie M. had worn a few minutes earlier. "Thanks, Coach."

"Go get 'em, Carter."

Buoyed by the praise, Carter hustled out to the mound and took his warm-up pitches. When the first Burton batter came to the plate, Carter felt more focused than he ever had before. The heat, the humidity, the knowledge that Burton had many strong hitters—all that faded into the background as he took the signal from Ash, wound up, and threw.

"Strike!"

He threw again.

"Strike!"

And once more.

"Strike three!"

The batter returned to the third-base dugout. The second Burton player fared no better. The third connected but for a weak grounder that Peter, playing shortstop, scooped and sent to Keith at first.

"Three up, three down," Raj said. "That's a nice way to begin."

Unfortunately, Burton began that way, too, its pitcher sending Freddie, Keith, and Craig right back to the dugout.

The teams traded sides again. Carter's heartbeat sped up a notch now, because he knew the first batter he'd face that inning was Marco Bellini.

A well-built boy who stood a few inches taller than many of his peers, Bellini gave off an aura of intimidation from the moment he stepped out of the dugout. He walked with the grace of an athlete and moved to the batter's box with a confidence few others showed.

Carter watched him from under the brim of his cap. Every inch of him wanted to take the ball from his glove and hurl it back in, over and over. But Liam had encouraged him to control that habit, pointing out that it could advertise to batters that he was nervous. So instead, he took a deep breath in, let it out slowly, and stared down at the plate.

Ash flashed the signal for a knuckleball. Carter nodded, making sure to keep his face blank. But inside, he was psyched. He hadn't thrown the knuckleball since the game against Pine Ridge. If Bellini hadn't seen him throw it then, it was possible he didn't know Carter had it in his arsenal.

Well, if Bellini didn't know about it before, he sure will now!

He narrowed his eyes and adjusted his grip so his fingertips were digging into the seams.

Bellini hefted the bat over his shoulders and gave it a slight twirl.

Carter reared back and hurled the ball. His delivery was perfect. The ball seemed to jiggle as it followed a path straight toward Ash's glove. Bellini took a monster cut at it—and missed by a mile.

Astonishment flickered across the slugger's face for a brief second. Then it was replaced by determination. That determination translated into a hit on the next throw that sent the ball right back at Carter. But the blast didn't have Bellini's usual power. Without flinching, Carter stuck out his glove and snared the ball for out number one.

Carter faced Bellini twice more in the innings that followed. Both times, he struck out the slugger with his knuckleball. Both times, those strikeouts ended Burton's turn at bat. After the second, Carter was certain he could see frustration etched on the faces of all the Burton players. He could understand why: So far, Forest

Park had prevented the high-scoring team from earning a single run!

Burton had returned the favor, however. If Forest Park didn't get on the board its last turn at bat, the championship would go into extra innings. Carter wouldn't be on the mound then, as he had hit eighty-five pitches with his last strike to Bellini, the highest number allowable in a game at his age. If Forest Park had to take to the field again, he'd be watching from the bench.

The sun was dipping toward the horizon when Craig, first up for Forest Park, grounded out. Then Charlie M. got on base with a single. That brought up Ash.

Carter had never seen his friend look so tense. He closed his eyes, unable to watch.

Crack!

His eyes flew open. He'd been squeezing them shut so tightly, he saw spots. For an endless moment he couldn't see the ball.

Then he did. It was coming down out of the darkening sky—and dropping behind the fence!

"Home run!"

CHAPTER NINETEEN

Liam sagged back against his bed's headboard and pulled out his earbuds. "They did it!" he murmured happily. "Forest Park is the State champs!"

As much as he had enjoyed listening to Carter's semifinal game with his teammates, he'd decided he wanted to be alone when he tuned in to the final. He couldn't explain why, not even to himself.

"Maybe you could picture the action better without the distractions," his mother suggested when he told her about it. Then she smiled gently. "Or maybe, after weeks of being with your friends, you just wanted a few hours alone. I think we all feel that way sometimes. I know I do."

Liam hoped to talk with Carter that night but then remembered that the Joneses would be traveling back home and that Carter would likely fall asleep on the way. Sure enough, he received a text from his cousin at nine thirty that night—twelve thirty Pennsylvania time.

2 tired 2 talk now, it read.

A second one followed immediately afterward. *Now it's your turn, doofus. BOL!*

Ravenna faced the Southern California North champions, Hollyhock, at eleven o'clock Saturday morning. The team had anticipated a hard-fought battle, but to the players' surprise, Hollyhock offered little resistance. Ravenna won 10–2.

And when it beat Hollyhock on Sunday as well by as wide a margin, Ravenna was bound for the Western Regional Tournament in San Bernardino.

Immediately after the game, the Ravenna players posed for their team photo behind the championship banner and received their State champs trading pins.

Coach Driscoll asked them all to gather in the dugout. "Sean, Owen, you can join us if you wish. You, too, Melanie, and, yes, you may bring your camera."

He waited until they were seated on the bench, then he stood before them, hands pressed together under his chin. Liam had expected a brief congratulatory speech, but instead Coach Driscoll began to tell a story.

"Many years ago, there was a boy who loved baseball. He played on Little League teams and tried his best every day. But the truth was, he just wasn't that good."

"Hey, Dad, what's the kid's name?"

Sean's question earned him an elbow in the ribs from his brother. "Idiot. He's talking about himself."

Coach Driscoll smiled and nodded. "I am. But even though I wasn't good, I still loved the game. I learned everything I could about it: player stats, team records, history, situational tactics, you name it. I remember everything, too." He tapped the side of his head. "Walking baseball encyclopedia, that's what I am."

"Can we quiz you?" Cole Dudley asked.

The coach laughed. "Maybe on the road trip to San Bernardino. But what I'm trying to say is this: that little boy never dreamed he'd grow up to coach a team like this one day. It is a pleasure and an honor to be your coach"—he paused for a moment to clear his throat, which seemed to have become a bit choked all of a sudden—"and I am looking forward to seeing just how far we can go on this journey to Williamsport."

Liam jumped up. "I'll tell you how far we're going! We're going all the way!"

His teammates leaped up, too. "All the way! All the way!" they chanted. "All the way!"

Back home that night, Liam and Carter finally found time to video-chat. Carter's first words had Liam cracking up.

"Winner! Winner! Chicken dinner!" his cousin cried the moment the connection was established.

"Man, if I had a nickel for every time I heard that," Liam said, still laughing, "I'd—"

"—be a millionaire," they finished together.

"Seriously, though, doofus, that's awesome!" Carter said. "Tell Rodney congrats for me. Did you catch any of my last game?"

"I heard the whole thing."

Carter raised an eyebrow. "Anything you want me to pass along to any of my teammates?"

Liam rolled his eyes. "Okay, fine. Tell Ash congratulations from me for that clutch home run."

Carter feigned astonishment. "Hang on just a minute. Did you just call him *Ash*?"

"Yeah, yeah, yeah," Liam grumbled good-naturedly. "I got tired of you correcting me all the time."

The two chatted for a long time, cracking jokes and

relating anecdotes of their experiences during their tournaments. When Carter told Liam what the Pine Ridge coach had said about him, Liam gave a low whistle of appreciation.

"Dude, you gotta take that one to the bank, because a compliment like that is money!"

Carter shook his head. "Yeah, I don't even know what that means." He gave a huge, face-splitting yawn then. "Listen, doofus, I gotta go. We have a ton of stuff to do tomorrow to get ready for Regionals."

"Gotcha. Same here," Liam replied. "Good luck, man." He held up his fist to the screen.

Carter's expression darkened slightly. It was such a brief flash of emotion that no one but Liam would likely have noticed it. But Liam did—and he instantly understood what caused it.

"Carter," he said soberly. "I am so sorry I did the fist-bump with Phillip. That's been our special thing so, yeah. Really, really sorry."

Carter looked away from the camera and scratched the back of his head. "Um, listen, don't worry about it. Because, actually, I have something to confess, too. A little while back I ran into Ash when I was about to take Lucky Boy for a walk in the woods." Lucky Boy was Carter's dog. The woods behind Carter's neighborhood was the one place he was allowed to roam free without a leash.

"Okay, so?" Liam prodded.

"So," Carter said, "I showed Ash the hideout."

The hideout was a natural rock overhang in the woods. Liam and Carter had discovered it when they were seven years old. They'd kept it a secret from everyone they knew, including their parents. Over the years it had become their getaway, a place they could go when they needed to talk about important stuff.

Liam had paid his last visit to the hideout months before. Carter had promised to keep the overhang their secret. Hearing that Carter hadn't kept his word was like getting a slap in the face. The hurt must have registered in his expression, because Carter quickly offered a fumbling apology and explanation.

"I'm sorry, Liam. It's just that Ash seemed really down about something. Once we got there, he kept asking me about Dad and our relationship and—see, he doesn't have a father and—oh, never mind. I messed up and I'm sorry."

"What do you mean he doesn't have a father? Are his parents divorced or did his dad die or what?"

Carter bit his lip. "I—I don't know. I never asked."

Liam shook his head. "Dude, the guy's your friend. Stuff like that? It's important."

Carter looked miserable. "There just was never the right time—"

"You got a six-hour bus ride to Bristol, right? There's your time. Ask."

CHAPTER

We'll see you in a few days," Mrs. Jones whispered in Carter's ear as she gave him one last hug.

It was early Wednesday morning. Carter, his teammates, and the coaches were boarding the chartered bus that would take them to Bristol, Connecticut, site of the Mid-Atlantic and New England Regional Tournaments. The ride would take six hours, landing them at their destination in the early afternoon.

"Pretty comfy," Ash commented as he slipped into the seat next to Carter.

Carter gave a short laugh. "Trust me: They stop being comfy at about hour three."

The players were very boisterous at the start of

their journey, talking and joking loudly. Soon, however, portable music players, gaming devices, and cell phones came out of pockets. As earbuds were nestled into ears, the chatter dropped to the occasional low murmur.

Carter stole a glance at Ash. His seatmate was plugged into his cell phone, nodding his head in time to some unheard music.

Go on, Carter urged himself.

Liam's admonishment had hit home. He knew Liam was right: The bus was the perfect time to ask Ash about his father. And if Ash didn't want to talk then...well, at least he'd know Carter was willing to listen.

He nudged Ash with his elbow. Ash opened his eyes and took out an earbud. "What's up? You need to use the bathroom?"

"Uh, no. Not yet, anyway." When Ash continued to look at him expectantly, Carter decided to just jump in feetfirst. "Ash, where's your dad?"

Ash's jaw dropped. For a moment Carter thought he'd stepped over a line in their friendship. Then to his great relief, Ash started laughing.

"Jeez, took you long enough to ask," he said. "Usually, it's the first thing people want to know about me— after my name, that is."

"Maybe I was trying to respect your privacy," Carter said defensively. "But now that I've asked..." He made a rotating motion with his hand, indicating that Ash should start talking.

"It's no big deal," Ash said. "My dad's in the military. He's gone a lot, sometimes even as long as a year."

Carter's eyes widened. "When's the last time you saw him?"

"Oh, we video-chat a bunch, so I see him that way. But in person?" Ash shook his head. "Been since last Thanksgiving."

"So he's never even seen where you live or the Diamond Champs or anything?" The Diamond Champs was an indoor baseball facility Ash's mother had purchased and renovated last winter. Carter, Ash, and their friends were frequent visitors there, particularly on rainy days.

"Again, not in person," Ash said in reply to Carter's question.

"When will you see him again—in person, I mean?"

Ash fiddled with his earbuds. "I'm not sure. Sometimes he thinks he'll be able to come home, but then..." He shrugged and put his earbuds back in, a clear signal that the conversation was over.

Carter turned his head and stared out the window.

He tried to imagine what it would be like not seeing his dad every day. Even now, knowing that they'd be apart until his parents arrived in Bristol for the tournament made him sad.

He must have dozed off for a while after that because the next thing he knew, the bus was stopping at a fast-food restaurant for lunch. Ordering and eating took an hour, then everyone piled back on the bus.

Two hours after that, they arrived at the A. Bartlett Giamatti Little League Leadership Training Center, site of the upcoming Regional tournaments. Named after the seventh commissioner of Major League Baseball, the complex was less than twenty-five years old and included a huge dining hall, a recreation building, and dormitories with bunk beds for the players. When not hosting the tournaments, the complex was used to train Little League coaches, umpires, and volunteers, among other things.

Though the boys on the bus were curious about the facility, what they really wanted to see was the baseball stadium: the Leon J. Breen Memorial Field. Many of them had watched the previous year's Mid-Atlantic Championship on national television. They'd seen the new and improved turf and been told the outfield fences had been pushed back, making a home run more difficult but that much more rewarding to achieve.

Now they would be playing on the same field they'd seen on TV.

"There it is! There it is!" Raj cried, spotting the field in the distance. When the bus continued moving, he added, "Aaaand there it goes. Come on, Coach, can't we stop and see it?"

"All in good time," Coach Harrison promised. "But first, let's get to the center so we can check in, okay?"

Hours later Carter was trying to get to sleep. He wasn't having any success. It wasn't that his bed was uncomfortable—he'd chosen the top bunk, with Ash on the bottom—it was that just as he would start to drift off, one of the boys would cough, or roll over, or make some other noise that jarred him back awake.

Same thing happened last year, he remembered. Back then he'd taken the bottom bunk and Liam had been above. He remembered, too, looking up that first night to see Liam leaning over the edge with a big grin on his face.

"What?" Carter had whispered as quietly as he could.

"We made it to Regionals!" Liam had whispered back. "I told you, didn't I? We're going to go all the way!"

Staring at the ceiling now, Carter felt a stab of homesickness. Such feelings had been hitting him throughout the afternoon, as he walked through hallways he'd last walked through with Liam; dined in the hall where he'd eaten meals with Liam; played Ping-Pong in the rec room where he and Liam had partnered up against all others; and even when he brushed his teeth, using the same sink he and Liam had both spit into the year before. He knew he would be making all new memories in the days ahead, meeting kids from all over New England and the Mid-Atlantic. He just wished he had someone to share those memories with, and to stand with him when he introduced himself to people he didn't know.

Suddenly, he felt a tap through the mattress beneath him.

"Hey, Carter, you awake?" Ash whispered.

Carter leaned over the side of his bunk and looked down. "Yeah. What's up?"

"You are!" Ash broke into a huge smile at his own joke.

Carter groaned. "That's as lame as one Liam or Rachel would tell," he whispered.

"Yeah. One more thing," Ash said.

"What?"

"We made it to Regionals!"

Carter grinned. "I know. Now go to sleep."

He rolled back onto his own pillow and, still smiling, closed his eyes. The night noises didn't bother him again.

CHAPTER
TWENTY-ONE

Hey, did you bring your collection?" Liam asked Rodney.

It was Thursday, and they were sitting together on a bus along with their teammates and coaches. The bus was bound for San Bernardino, California, site of the Western and Northwest Regional Tournaments. Southern California, or SoCal as it was often abbreviated, was playing its first game of the Western Regional Tournament at nine o'clock Saturday morning.

Rodney gave him a confused look. "My collection of what?"

"Your trading pins!" Liam replied impatiently. Then it occurred to him that he'd never actually seen Rodney with a pin bag or any pins other than the ones he received for participating in a tournament. "You trade them, right?"

Rodney just shrugged.

"Well, then what do you do with them?" Liam demanded to know.

"I've been sticking them in my sock drawer," Rodney replied. "Why? What am I supposed to do with them?"

Liam stood up and, bracing himself in case the bus suddenly lurched, grabbed his backpack from the carrier above his head. He sat back down, pulled out his pin bag, and opened it up.

"Holy cow!" Rodney stared in amazement at the vast assortment of colorful metal displayed on Liam's lap. Other players looked over their seat backs or crowded into empty spots nearby to see the collection, too. "Where'd you get all those?"

"Carter and I have been collecting and trading for years," Liam said. "His is just as good."

He touched an unusual one that featured images of two well-known video game characters and the famous Olympic rings. "I got this one last year at the Little League Baseball World Series from a kid from China. It's from the Summer Olympics. Neither of us understood a word the other was saying, but it didn't matter.

He had a pin I liked, I had one he liked, so we traded. It's one of my favorites. Then there's this one."

Liam pointed to a more plain one that showed a simple orange-and-brown baseball diamond and the words *Little League Baseball Division* in gold print. "It belonged to my dad when he was a kid. He gave it to me to start my collection. I'd never trade it or the Olympic one away."

He looked up at Rodney. "How have you never heard of this? It's a huge deal, especially at the World Series! People come from all over to trade."

"Do you have a collection?" Rodney asked Phillip.

Phillip nodded.

"Do you all have one?" Rodney asked the group at large.

Everyone nodded.

"How have I never heard of this?" Rodney wondered aloud.

Liam selected a pin from his bag and handed it to his friend. "There. Now you won't go into it empty-handed. But after the tournament, make sure to get something like this bag to put your own pins in so you can take them with you when we go to Williamsport."

Rodney raised his eyebrows. "You seem pretty sure we're going to make it there."

Liam shook his head. "No, not pretty sure. Absolutely positive!"

"What's it like there, anyway? Did you ever get, I don't know, homesick or anything?" The questions came from Matt. He was a big guy and one of Ravenna's most consistent hitters. Usually, he exuded confidence. Now, though, he was chewing on his thumbnail and looking nervous.

Liam exchanged glances with Phillip. An unspoken agreement passed between them.

"What's it like?" Liam echoed. "It's unbelievably fun."

"Baseball is the center attraction, of course," Phillip contributed, "but there's a rec room with video games, a huge pool—"

"—and Ping-Pong tables—" Liam added.

"—and the food is awesome!" Phillip finished.

Matt's thumb left his mouth. "Sounds pretty good," he said with a hint of a grin.

"Best. Time. Ever," Liam said. "Seriously."

The conversation ended then because the bus stopped to fuel up. Everyone was allowed off the bus to stretch his legs.

Coach Driscoll approached Liam and beckoned to Phillip. "I overheard you talking to Matt," he said in a low voice. "It made me realize that you two are in a unique position as the only ones on our team to have experienced Regionals and the World Series." He glanced over his shoulder. "Some of these boys have never been out of the San Fernando Valley before. Some haven't even been away from their families overnight. A few parents have contacted me to express their concern that their children might have trouble." He spread his hands wide. "I'll do everything I can to put those boys at ease, but I'm hoping you might help, too. They might be more comfortable asking you questions than me. And, frankly, you'd probably have better answers, too." He smiled.

Liam was more than willing to help out, and he told the coach as much. So did Phillip. Then they all boarded the bus to resume the journey.

An hour later, they pulled onto the road leading to the Western Region Headquarters.

"Cool!" Liam said, staring out the window. "Look at those giant baseballs!"

Lining the edge of the parking area next to the street were enormous concrete baseballs and softballs.

"They call them 'bollards,'" Phillip informed his teammates as the bus rolled past and headed into the main lot in front of the headquarters entrance. "I think they're there to stop vandals from getting into the lot.

Anyway, each one was donated. My family bought one after we won the Little League Baseball World Series last year," he added proudly. "It's got a plaque on it and everything."

"No way," Christopher said. "I want to see."

"Me, too. Can we, Dad?" Rodney asked.

When Coach Driscoll gave them permission, Phillip led the way to the proper ball. "See? Told you!"

Christopher stepped forward and read the plaque out loud. "'Donated by the DiMaggio family.' Then there's a long list of names including Phillip's." Suddenly, he gave a yelp. He looked at the plaque, then at Phillip, and then back to the plaque. "There's another name here, too. Joseph P. DiMaggio!"

Phillip nodded. "Oh, yeah. He was my great-grandfath—wait a minute." He started laughing. "You're thinking Joseph P. DiMaggio is *the* Joe DiMaggio, the great Yankee player from the 1940s, aren't you? Well, sorry to burst your bubble, but the *P* in his name stood for *Paul*. Joseph *Paul* DiMaggio was Joltin' Joe, the Yankee Clipper." He pointed at the plaque. "The *P* in that name stands for *Phillip*. That's where I get my name from."

Liam's jaw dropped. "So your great-grandfather's name really was Joe DiMaggio?"

"Yeah." A look of understanding crossed Phillip's

face. "Oh my gosh! I didn't really lie to Carter that time in baseball camp after all. Of course, I still shouldn't have let him think Grandpa Joe was *the* Joe. And I shouldn't have played that prank on him. If I had told him the truth and been a little nicer, none of this would have happened." He touched his chest, then his nose, and then pointed at Liam.

Liam laughed. "True. But if that hadn't happened, then maybe neither of us would have worked as hard as we did to improve. And if we hadn't, then maybe none of this"—he gestured to the facility around him—"would have happened either. So in the long run—"

"—it all worked out," Phillip finished.

CHAPTER
TWENTY-TWO

Whoa, check out all the teams!" Raj exclaimed. "And look! There's Dugout!"

It was Friday evening, and Forest Park had just arrived at the Leon J. Breen stadium for the Opening Ceremony parade. Dugout, the Little League mascot, was at the front, ready to lead the teams onto the field. Besides Forest Park, there were five other State champs from the Mid-Atlantic region: New Jersey, New York, Delaware, District of Columbia, and Maryland. The remaining six teams were from New England: Massachusetts, Rhode Island, Connecticut, New Hampshire, Vermont, and Maine. Each team carried its State Championship banner. The players were dressed in their uniforms, forming a rippling ribbon of kaleidoscopic colors as they marched onto the field.

"Whoa," Carter heard Raj say, "look at all the *people!*"

The stands were packed with spectators, all of whom were on their feet cheering and clapping as the teams processed before them. Once everyone was inside, two players, one from Vermont, the other from Maryland, stepped up to a microphone. They had been selected to lead the others in reciting the Little League pledge.

Next, a young woman recited the Little League Parent and Volunteer pledge on behalf of all the adults involved. Carter saw Coach Harrison mouthing the words as they were spoken: *I will teach all children to play fair and do their best. I will positively support all managers, coaches and players. I will respect the decisions of the umpires. I will praise a good effort despite the outcome of the game.*

The coach caught him watching and gave him a wink. Carter grinned and then turned his attention back to the activities. He cheered as several "first pitches" were thrown by brave men and women who had led rescue efforts in a coastal town nearly swept away by an enormous flood. He listened politely to speeches by the Little League regional director and his assistant director, and then to one by the mayor of Bristol. Her speech praised a former Connecticut Little Leaguer who had become a doctor and now traveled the world helping heal communities stricken with disease.

The ceremonies ended with loud roars and music. Carter was thrilled to be part of it all. But for him, the real excitement started at two o'clock the next day. That's when Forest Park faced the District of Columbia for its first game of the tournament.

"Weird how DC is considered a state, huh?" Stephen commented to Carter in the dugout after their warm-ups. He chattered on for a few more minutes about how the name "Columbia" was the way people in the 1700s referred to the United States, "because, of course, it wasn't called the United States then."

Carter figured Stephen was trying to cover up his nervousness and let him talk without interruption. He hoped the first baseman would relax soon, though.

He was a bit jumpy himself, but he calmed as soon as he hit the field. He was playing third base that game, not pitching. He didn't see much action in the hot corner the first two innings, but in the third he sparked a spectacular play.

The score was Pennsylvania 3, DC 1. DC had runners at first and second, no outs. The batter stepped into the box.

He's going to bunt, Carter thought. He glanced at

Coach Harrison for confirmation. Sure enough, the coach made a revolving motion with his hand, his signal to put a "wheel" style defense in play.

When the batter squared to bunt, the Forest Park players were already in motion. Allen raced from short to cover third. Freddie readied himself at second. Stephen was on first. Carter charged in to field the bunt.

Thock!

The ball rebounded off the bat and hit the grass. But it didn't stop after a few feet, as the batter undoubtedly hoped. Rather, the ball dribbled right toward Carter!

Carter didn't bother to put a glove on it. Instead, he barehanded the ball, spun, and flipped it to Allen. Allen stepped on third.

One out.

Allen rifled the ball to Freddie, who swept his glove down and tagged the runner sliding in from first.

Two outs.

And, amazingly, Freddie's throw to first almost beat the batter. If it had, Forest Park would have had a triple play! As it was, DC got out a moment later, when its batter hit a weak grounder to Luke on the mound. Luke fired the ball to Stephen—and that was that.

Three innings and two runs later, Pennsylvania had

its first win of the tournament. It added a second the next evening with a hard-fought victory over a tough team from New York.

Carter didn't pitch that game and played only three of the six innings. He was slotted to pitch Tuesday, and even though Forest Park didn't play Monday, Coach Harrison wanted to be sure his arm was fully rested.

That night after dinner and a long visit with his parents, Carter found a quiet spot outside under a tree. The orange and pink sunset was splashed across the horizon, looking as if it had been painted by a giant's broad brush. He took a couple of photos with his phone and sent the best of them to Liam with a short text: *Bet the Left Coast doesn't look like this!*

Liam replied instantly: *Course not, dork. It's only 4:30!*

Carter started to text back but stopped when his phone rang. He grinned and answered, "Hey, doofus! How's things in the West?"

"Things could not be better," Liam boomed. "We won both games so far!"

"Us, too!" Carter was happy to report. "We're off tomorrow, and then we play again on Tuesday."

"Us, too!" Liam echoed. "What're you going to do with your free time?"

"The usual," Carter replied. "Swim, video games, eat, Ping-Pong."

"Yeah, that's what I'm planning to do, too. Who're you partnering with?"

"Ash. You?"

Liam chuckled. "Phillip. Weird, huh?"

Carter laughed softly. "Totally. Hey, we'll have to play each other if..." He let his voice trail off, worried if he actually said the words "we both make it to Williamsport" out loud, he might jinx his team.

Liam knew what he meant, of course. "Not if, dork. When."

The boys chatted for a while longer. Then the mosquitoes started attacking Carter with such viciousness he had to end the call. "Talk to you soon," he said.

"*See* you soon," Liam responded. "Like in a week!"

CHAPTER
TWENTY-THREE

After hanging up with Carter, Liam stood, stretched, and went in search of Phillip and the other Ravenna players. He found them in the recreation room watching a movie. Kids from other teams were there, too.

"Hey, any of you guys want to play some Ping-Pong?" The invitation came from a stocky boy with a buzz cut so severe Liam could see more scalp than hair. Another boy, with smooth dark skin, glossy black hair, and braces, was slapping a paddle against his thigh. The two were obviously partners.

Liam nudged Phillip. "Want to take them on?"

Phillip pulled himself up out of the deep, cushioned

seat of his easy chair. "Definitely. This movie is boring. Plus, I've seen it three times."

Buzz Cut introduced himself and his partner. "I'm Mike Worley, and this is Diego Rochester. We're on the team from Little Lake, Idaho. You're from Ravenna, SoCal, right?"

As Liam nodded, he felt Diego's eyes on him.

"You look really familiar, you know that?" Diego said. He jerked his chin at Phillip. "I know who you are because I watched the Little League Baseball World Series last year." He looked back at Liam. "But you . . ."

Suddenly, he snapped his fingers. "You were there, too, weren't you? Oh, no way! Mike, you know who this is?"

Mike gave a huge shrug that made his neck disappear between his shoulders.

"It's the kid from Pennsylvania who struck out in the U.S. Championship! In fact, you"—Diego jerked his chin at Phillip again—"were the one who struck him out." He stared at Liam in consternation. "What the heck are you doing here?"

Before Liam could reply, Phillip slammed his Ping-Pong paddle down on the table. "I'll tell you what he's doing here!" he said hotly. "He's here because he's a great player, a great catcher, a great hitter, and a great teammate, that's what! And if you have a problem—"

"Whoa, whoa, whoa!" Diego held up his hands in surrender. "I meant, what is he doing here in *California*? Of course he's a great player or else he wouldn't be here!" He pointed at the ground to indicate the Western Regional Tournament.

"Oh. Sorry." Phillip picked up his paddle again. "He moved here last year. Now, you guys ready to play?"

The three other boys regarded him for a long moment. Then they all started laughing. "Yeah, we're ready."

Liam and Phillip lost to the Idahoans two games out of three. Then it was time for dinner. They parted company, but not before Liam challenged Mike and Diego to a rematch later in the week.

Mike's face fell then. "I don't know if we'll be here still," he mumbled. "We lost one of our games already."

Eight teams annually represent the United States during the month of August in the Little League Baseball World Series played at Little League International in South Williamsport, PA. These teams are determined each summer by participation in the world's largest elimination tournament. State champions from forty-nine states (one champion from the Dakotas) participate in eight Little League Baseball Regional tournaments hosted by Little League's five regional centers in the United States. Two Regional champions (West and Northwest) are decided at the Western Region Headquarters in San Bernardino, CA; two (New England and Mid-Atlantic) at the Eastern Region Headquarters in Bristol, CT; and two (Midwest and Great Lakes) at the Central Region Headquarters in Indianapolis, IN. The Southeast Region Headquarters (Warner Robins, GA) and the Southwest Region Headquarters (Waco, TX) host tournaments that produce a single Regional champion to complete the United States bracket in the Little League Baseball World Series.

Liam reminded Mike that losing one game wasn't the end of Idaho's journey. He didn't think his words had much effect, though. When Mike left with Diego, he was looking glum.

Since he wasn't playing the next day, Liam made a point of attending Idaho's game. He cheered for his new friends and was happy for them when they won.

"Maybe we'll get that rematch in after all," Mike said when Liam ran into him later on his way to the cages for batting practice.

"Yeah, if not here, then maybe next week, huh?"

Mike showed crossed fingers on both hands and

then headed off to celebrate with his teammates. Liam continued to the batting cages.

"Okay, boys, grab a bat and get to work," Coach Driscoll said when the players were assembled.

Liam adjusted his gloves, made sure his helmet was straight, and took up his position in the box.

Foomp! The pitching machine shot the first ball toward him. *Whack!* He blasted a line drive. For the next few minutes those two sounds plus the sound of his breathing were all he heard. When the machine had emptied, he stepped out.

"Nice work, Liam," Coach Driscoll said. "Didn't miss one. Think you can do the same in the game tomorrow?"

Liam smiled. "If they come at me nice and straight like those pitches did? No problem! If not"—he shrugged—"can't promise I won't miss occasionally, but I can promise to do my best."

"That's all I can ask for."

Cole trotted up to them then. "Excuse me, Coach, when is the game tomorrow night? I told my folks eight. Is that right?"

The coach confirmed that it was.

Liam was glad for the late start for two reasons. One, it meant they wouldn't be playing under the glare of the hot California sun but rather beneath the stadium lights. And two, it meant he could tune in to Carter's game, which started at five o'clock Connecticut time, two o'clock California time. He mentioned his plan to Rodney and Phillip that night at dinner. Both said they'd like to listen to the game as well.

So the next day after lunch, the threesome snagged chairs in the rec room, located the stream of the Mid-Atlantic Regional Tournament, and settled in to watch the action.

"Carter's pitching?" Rodney asked.

Liam nodded.

Rodney snuggled himself deeper in his chair. "Then this should be good."

CHAPTER
TWENTY-FOUR

Carter leaned in, ball behind his back, and stared down at the batter. It was a look he practiced in the mirror from time to time: eyes narrowed, expression confident, and lips set with determination. It was aimed at intimidating.

Good thing they can't see the butterflies in my stomach, he thought.

It was the top of the first inning of the Pennsylvania-Maryland game. Maryland had lost both of its previous contests, but Carter knew better than to anticipate an easy victory. Rather, he believed Maryland would come out fighting, the way a cornered animal will go on the offensive to stay alive.

Ash flashed the signal for a changeup. Carter gave a curt nod and went into his windup. He threw.

Crack! Carter's heart fell when Maryland's leadoff batter connected on his very first pitch. But then it leaped again when he saw the path the ball was taking. It traced a high arc into the air above left field. Charlie M. had plenty of time to get under it. Standing with the glove raised and ready, he caught the ball easily for out number one.

Still, Carter thought. *I got lucky.*

He pitched carefully to the next batter and struck him out. The third Maryland hopeful grounded out to end the inning.

"Freddie! Keith! Craig!" Coach Filbert called out.

While Freddie stood up to prepare for his turn at bat, Ash had a brief conversation with Coach Filbert. Then he slipped onto the bench next to Carter.

"Coach says their cleanup batter has been pretty successful this tournament," he said in a low voice, "and so we should try out the you-know-what."

Carter nodded. "Okay."

They turned their attention to Freddie, who had just stepped up to the plate.

Freddie watched two pitches go by for balls. The third was a called strike. He swung at the fourth and connected for a high pop-up. The Maryland shortstop took two steps back and caught it.

Keith fared better. He knocked a grounder that drove between first and second and beat the throw. Craig followed up that single with one of his own. That brought up Charlie M. Charlie had been a force to contend with at the plate in the last two games. He was again now.

Crack! He blasted a double to shallow left field. A roar of approval rose from the stands as Keith rounded third, raced home, and scored. Craig, however, was thrown out at third.

"Here goes nothing," Ash quipped as he headed to the plate. Unfortunately, "nothing" is what his turn at bat yielded. He struck out to end the inning.

Carter hurried to the mound. He couldn't wait to get the signal for the knuckleball. But when he looked down at the first batter, he nearly fell over with surprise.

It was a girl!

He recovered quickly. Girls had been playing in Little League for decades—his friend Rachel was a strong player—but even so, Carter hadn't expected to face one at Regionals. He wondered why Ash hadn't warned him that the Maryland player was a girl.

There can only be one reason, he figured. *Ash didn't know, either!*

He knew one thing for sure, though. If Coach Filbert had instructed them to use the knuckleball on her, he must have believed the girl was capable of hitting his fastball and changeup.

Carter leaned in, took the signal for the knuckleball, reared back, and threw.

The girl swung and missed by a mile. She quickly stepped out of the box, looking a bit bewildered. The look lasted for only a moment, though. When she got back into her stance, her expression was fierce.

It didn't help. Two more knuckleballs, two more strikes, and the cleanup hitter was walking back to her dugout.

Carter and his teammates allowed just two hits that inning and no runs. Their turn at bat, they added three to their side of the board to make it Pennsylvania 4, Maryland 0. But Maryland wasn't about to roll over. It roared back with a three-run inning in the third to draw within one.

That's the way the score stayed until the top of the sixth. Then Maryland's cleanup batter did what Carter thought she'd never do. With a runner on second and one out courtesy of a sacrifice bunt, she hit his knuckle-ball deep into the gap between right and center fields.

Charlie S. raced in from one direction. Craig dashed in from the other. Neither got under the ball in time. Then they got in each other's way as they both scrambled to pick it up. Meanwhile, the batter was rounding second for third and the runner from second was heading home. By the time Craig and Charlie S. sorted themselves out, the runner had scored and the girl was at third, proud owner of an RBI triple.

She didn't move from that spot, however, for Carter struck out the next two to end the inning.

Pennsylvania 4, Maryland 4.

"Okay, boys," Coach Harrison said, clapping his hands together and bouncing on his toes. "This is it. Score now and we walk off winners. Don't score and we get to keep playing. Now, I love baseball as much as anyone else, but, personally, I'd rather end it now so we can get some dinner before it's really late. I hear they're serving pizza tonight!"

The promise of pizza might have motivated the boys in the regular season. But at Regionals, something else spurred them on. That something came from within each player. It was a combination of competitiveness, determination, and the desire to perform his best—not for personal glory, but for the sake of the team.

They stood in a circle and put their hands together in the middle. "Let's hear it!" Coach Harrison said.

"FOREST PARK, ONE-TWO-THREE! FOREST PARK, ONE-TWO-THREE!"

That cry, it turned out, came from a team of winners. Six batters and one run later, Pennsylvania defeated Maryland.

CHAPTER
TWENTY-FIVE

Liam strode to the plate. Before he stepped into the batter's box, he scooped up a handful of dirt, rubbed it on the palms of his gloves, and then brushed the excess off. He adjusted his helmet. Finally, he took up his position next to the plate.

It was his first at bat of the game against Northern California, and he wanted to be sure everything was just right.

When Liam had first learned that the enormous state sent two representatives to Regionals, he had assumed that there'd be a bitter rivalry between North and South. He'd feared that such a rivalry might cast a negative cloud over their game. But he soon discovered he was wrong. While the game was one of the most antic-ipated of the tournament, its popularity was mostly due to the fact that the players on both sides were considered "local boys." In the end, they were all Californians.

Two hours earlier Liam heard that spectators were circling the streets in their cars, looking for open spaces to park. He realized that the Al Houghton Stadium might be packed to capacity with more than seven thou-sand fans. He also realized that many of his teammates had never played in front of such a huge crowd before and so might be intimidated.

Worried, he grabbed Phillip and explained his concern.

"We've got to make sure they're relaxed and ready," he said. "Any ideas?"

Phillip thought for a moment. Then he nodded. "Got one." Phillip quickly rounded up the other players. "Okay, here's the deal. If any of you feel like you're start-ing to tighten up out there, I want you to visualize this."

He shot Liam a significant look, then took a step back and stuck his arms out to his sides. Then, to Liam's great amusement, he started waving them up and down, waggling his hips, and chanting, "Loosey-goosey! Loosey-goosey!"

The Ravenna players cracked up.

Phillip grinned. "I know: I look ridiculous, right? But I'm willing to give it everything I've got, even my self-respect, if it helps us win."

Liam wasn't thinking about that image now, however. He was completely focused on the pitcher. In the first inning, the NoCal hurler had thrown a combination of fastballs and changeups that had proved hard to hit. Hard, but not impossible. SoCal had gotten on the board with a run thanks to an RBI double off Rodney's bat.

Now, at the top of the second inning, Liam wondered what he'd see coming toward him.

The pitcher bent forward and nodded his agreement with his catcher's signal. He straightened, wound up, and, with a lunging step forward, threw.

Liam tried to track the ball's path as it flew toward him. But he couldn't. The ball bobbled through the air with a jiggling, dancing motion that his eyes found impossible to follow.

Thud!

"Strike!"

Twice more, the NoCal pitcher threw the erratic pitch. Twice more, Liam stood next to the plate like a house at the side of the road, unmoving and locked in place.

"Strike three!" the umpire cried.

Liam still didn't move.

"Son, I'm sorry, but you're out. Please return to your dugout," the umpire said not unkindly.

Liam shook himself and trudged back to the bench, still holding his bat. He sat staring at the ground.

Rodney eased up next to him. "Hey, don't worry about it," he said. "Everybody strikes out now and then."

Liam blinked and turned to look at his friend. "I know. That's not...I'm not..." He let out a frustrated huff of air, then took off his batting helmet and cap and raked his fingers through his brown hair. "That pitcher struck me out with knuckleballs."

Rodney nodded, puzzlement etched on his face.

"Carter throws knuckleballs," Liam said.

"Yeah. So?"

Liam took a deep breath in through his nose and let it out slowly through his mouth, a breathing technique Coach Driscoll had taught him that was supposed to help calm nerves. It didn't work.

"So," he answered at last, "what am I going to do if he's on the mound and I'm at the plate—and the U.S. Championship is on the line?"

He leaned forward and put his head in his hands. "I'll tell you what I'm going to do. I'm going to strike out. Again. And lose my team the chance to play in the Little League Baseball World Series. Again. And that strikeout will be caught on national television, seen by hundreds of thousands of people all over the world, and available on the Internet forever."

He moved his hands and let his head drop down.

"Again."

As he stared at the ground, he felt Rodney move away from him; someone else took Rodney's place. An arm draped over his shoulders, gave a quick squeeze, and then was removed. Liam looked up and found Coach Driscoll regarding him kindly.

"Liam," the coach said, "I'd like you to do something for me."

"Okay," Liam said slowly. "What?"

"I'd like you to be proud of yourself."

Liam's eyes widened.

"I'd like you to think back on this season," the coach continued. "Think of what you've accomplished. Of the challenges and the obstacles you've overcome. Of how you've helped get us here." Coach Driscoll swept an arm toward the diamond. "You made some mistakes in the regular season, but you didn't give up on yourself. You figured out what you needed to do to get back on course, and then you did it."

Crack!

Both the coach and Liam looked at the field. Phillip had just hit a bouncing grounder. Now he dropped the bat, ran for all he was worth, and beat the throw to first. The coach applauded with his players and then turned back to Liam.

"You didn't give up when you came face-to-face with Phillip, either," he said. "Instead, you broke through the wall between the two of you and held out your hand in friendship. That took real guts."

Liam flushed with a mixture of embarrassment and gratitude at the praise. "Thanks," he murmured.

"As for what may or may not happen between you and Carter in the future . . ." The coach shrugged. "We'll deal with that together if we make it to Williamsport."

Liam stared at him. Then he gave a smile that lit up his whole face.

"'If'? Don't you mean 'when'? Because I have to tell you, Coach"—he straightened, gazed around the dugout at his teammates, and said in a loud, clear voice—"we're going to go all the way!"

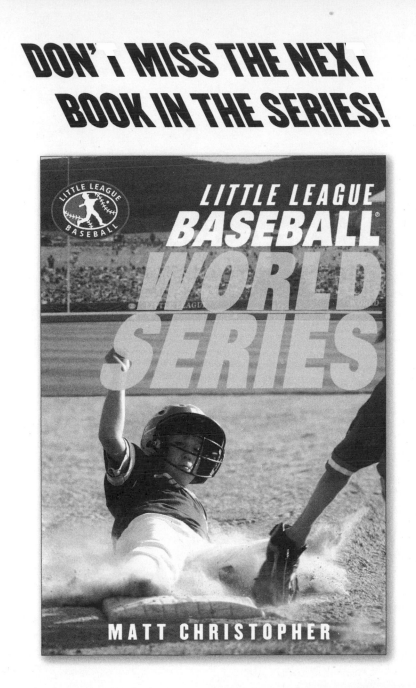

WHAT IS LITTLE LEAGUE®?

With nearly 165,000 teams in all 50 states and over 80 other countries across the globe, Little League Baseball® is the world's largest organized youth sports program! Many of today's Major League players started their baseball careers in Little League Baseball, including Derek Jeter, David Wright, Justin Verlander, and Adrian Gonzalez.

Little League® is a nonprofit organization that works to teach the principles of sportsmanship, fair play, and teamwork. Concentrating on discipline, character, and courage, Little League is focused on more than just developing athletes: It helps to create upstanding citizens.

Carl Stotz established Little League in 1939 in Williamsport, Pennsylvania. The first league only had three teams and played six innings, but by 1946, there were already twelve leagues throughout the state of Pennsylvania. The following year, 1947, was the first year that the Little League Baseball® World Series was played, and it has continued to be played every August since then.

In 1951, Little League Baseball expanded internationally, and the first permanent league to form outside of the United States was on each end of the Panama Canal. Little League Baseball later moved to nearby South Williamsport, Pennsylvania, and a second stadium, the Little League Volunteer Stadium, was opened in 2001.

Some key moments in Little League history:

- **1957**   The Monterrey, Mexico, team became the first international team to win the World Series.
- **1964**   Little League was granted a federal charter.
- **1974**   The federal charter was amended to allow girls to join Little League.
- **1982**   The Peter J. McGovern Little League Museum opened.
- **1989**   Little League introduced the Challenger Division.
- **2001**   The World Series expanded from eight to sixteen teams to provide a greater opportunity for children to participate in the World Series.
- **2014**   Little League will celebrate its 75th anniversary.

HOW DOES A LITTLE LEAGUE®
TEAM GET TO THE WORLD SERIES?

In order to play in the Little League Baseball® World Series, a player must first be a part of a regular-season Little League, and then be selected as part of their league's All-Star team, consisting of players ages 11 to 13 from any of the teams. The All-Star teams compete in District, Sectional, and State tournaments to become their State champions. The State champions then compete to represent one of eight different geographic regions of the United States (New England, Mid-Atlantic, Southeast, Great Lakes, Midwest, Northwest, Southwest, and West). All eight of the Regional tournament winners play in the Little League Baseball World Series.

The eight International Tournament winners (representing Asia-Pacific, Africa, Australia, Canada, the Caribbean, Europe, Mexico, Japan, and Latin America) also come to the Little League Baseball World Series.

The eight U.S. Regional Tournament winners compete in the United States Bracket of the Little League

Baseball World Series, and the International Tournament winners compete in the International Bracket.

Over eleven days, the Little League Baseball World Series proceeds until a winning U.S. Championship team and International Championship team are determined. The final World Series Championship Game is played between the U.S. Champions and the International Champions.

WANT TO LEARN MORE?

Visit the *World of Little League, Peter J. McGovern Museum, and Official Store* in South Williamsport, Pennsylvania! When you visit, you'll find pictures, interactive displays, films, and exhibits showing the history and innovations of Little League.

More information is available online at Little LeagueMuseum.org.

CALLING ALL SHARP-EYED READERS!
CAN YOU FIND THE WORDS LISTED BELOW?

BASEBALL

BAT

CARL E. STOTZ

CARTER

CATCHER'S MASK

CHAMPION

DOUBLE PLAY

FIRST BASE

GLOVE

HOME RUN

HOWARD J. LAMADE
STADIUM

LIAM

OUT

PHILLIP

PICKLE

PITCHER'S MOUND

PLAYERS

RUNNER ON BASE

SAFE

SLIDE

STRIKE

TOURNAMENT

TRIPLE

WORLD SERIES

All words are either vertical, horizontal, or diagonal (and even backwards in those directions)!

Answers on page 181.

```
M R A D P N S V Z S I E C L A C W R O T S P Z L U
O B X S K L O U S M E N T O U R N A M E N T I H P
H L V W I O B A T O L Z J P A N T W Q U B P I S R
O R D A P L N E S U M H G C Y N O I P M A H C H D
W Z M O M L B N E T T R F A C I S V L K O L A X H
A Q Y K S E V P H L N A H I L D M O L N D G R A S
R U N N E R O N B A S E G D R O Y X A B A J L Q U
D A W B R E K C I T O P N Y H S Z P B O M S E R T
J O C N V R U E N L K U V L X N T J E K I D S A C
L D H O Y M S B Z G O R E J U D G B S A O K T I N
A U T Y W P X I T M Q O K E M E D V A Y P P O M Z
M J A C Z T H U S F A T I U N R S L B S C B T I U
A H V E N W O R L D S E R I E S O C W I E J Z M Q
D L N P S R E S E F L Q T O X L A R O Z N J Y E H
E C R D A H I K W J I Y S N A T P Y B H T B S B J
S W O L C O S C Y V D O W R C R D I K Z G E L A P
T A G T H M K I G S E F W H O V E E R K P B O G U
A L I D N E A M T B R M E B Y A L T G T I U R L T
D P C B W R G X R I P R P U P S G H R N F R P O R
I O Z I V U L R O V S C H G B A S L G A X I N V M
U L D Q I N V C L M E P I J O F G H Y D C K O E F
M F T R B K L F A T T E L E S E D Q P K I P R F S
B U C V E T O S I D Q N L Y A L P E L B U O D W E
D R O W P U K M T H K L I G S R J E Y T H F M L L
A P L A Y E R S X F Z W P N G C O M A F W C V N Z
```

HOW CAN I JOIN A LITTLE LEAGUE® TEAM?

If you have access to the Internet, you can see if your community has a local league by going to LittleLeague.org and clicking on "Find a League." You can also visit one of our regional offices:

US REGIONAL OFFICES:
Western Region Headquarters (AK, AZ, CA, HI, ID, MT, NV, OR, UT, WA, and WY)
6707 Little League Drive
San Bernardino, CA 92407
E-MAIL: westregion@LittleLeague.org

Southwestern Region Headquarters (AR, CO, LA, MS, NM, OK, and TX)
3700 South University Parks Drive
Waco, TX 76706
E-MAIL: southwestregion@LittleLeague.org

Central Region Headquarters (IA, IL, IN, KS, KY, MI, MN, MO, ND, NE, OH, SD, and WI)
9802 E. Little League Drive
Indianapolis, IN 46235
E-MAIL: centralregion@LittleLeague.org

Southeastern Region Headquarters (AL, FL, GA, NC, SC, TN, VA, and WV)
PO Box 7557
Warner Robins, GA 31095
E-MAIL: southeastregion@LittleLeague.org

Eastern Region Headquarters (CT, DC, DE, MA, MD, ME, NH, NJ, NY, PA, RI, and VT)
PO Box 2926
Bristol, CT 06011
E-MAIL: eastregion@LittleLeague.org

INTERNATIONAL REGIONAL OFFICES:
CANADIAN REGION (serving all of Canada)
Canadian Little League Headquarters
235 Dale Avenue
Ottawa, ONT
Canada KIG OH6
E-MAIL: Canada@LittleLeague.org

ASIA-PACIFIC REGION (serving all of Asia and
Australia)
Asia-Pacific Regional Director
C/O Hong Kong Little League
Room 1005, Sports House
1 Stadium Path
Causeway Bay, Hong Kong
E-MAIL: bhc368@netvigator.com

EUROPE, MIDDLE EAST & AFRICA REGION
(serving all of Europe, the Middle East, and Africa)
Little League Europe
A1. Meleg Legi 1
Kutno, 99-300, Poland
E-MAIL: Europe@LittleLeague.org

LATIN AMERICA REGION (serving Mexico and Latin
American regions)
Latin America Little League Headquarters
PO Box 10237
Caparra Heights, Puerto Rico 00922-0237
E-MAIL: LatinAmerica@LittleLeague.org

```
M R A D P N S V Z S I E C L A C W R O T S P Z L U
O B X S K L O U S M E N T O U R N A M E N T I H P
H L V W I O B A T O L Z J P A N T W Q U B P I S R
O R D A P L N E S U M H G C Y N O I P M A H C H D
W Z M O M L B N E T T R F A C I S V L K O L A X H
A Q Y K S E V P H L N A H I L D M O L N D G R A S
R U N N E R O N B A S E G D R O Y X A B A J L Q U
D A W B R E K C I T O P N Y H S Z P B O M S E R T
J O C N V R U E N L K U V L X N T J E K I D S A C
L D H O Y M S B Z G O R E J U D G B S A O K T I N
A U T Y W P X I T M Q O K E M E D V A Y P P O M Z
M J A C Z T H U S F A T I U N R S L B S C B T I U
A H V E N W O R L D S E R I E S O C W I E J Z M Q
D L N P S R E S E F L Q T O X L A R O Z N J Y E H
E C R D A H I K W J I Y S N A T P Y B H T B S B J
S W O L C O S C Y V D O W R C R D I K Z G E L A P
T A G T H M K I G S E F W H O V E E R K P B O G U
A L I D N E A M T B R M E B Y A L T G T I U R L T
D P C B W R G X R I P R P U P S G H R N F R P O R
I O Z I V U L R O V S C H G B A S L G A X I N V M
U L D Q I N V C L M E P I J O F G H Y D C K O E F
M F T R B K L F A T T E L E S E D Q P K I P R F S
B U C V E T O S I D Q N L Y A L P E L B U O D W E
D R O W P U K M T H K L I G S R J E Y T H F M L L
A P L A Y E R S X F Z W P N G C O M A F W C V N Z
```